Samuel Mucklebackit

The Battles of Dunbar and Prestonpans

And other Selected Poems New and Old

Samuel Mucklebackit

The Battles of Dunbar and Prestonpans
And other Selected Poems New and Old

ISBN/EAN: 9783744769662

Printed in Europe, USA, Canada, Australia, Japan

Cover: Foto ©Andreas Hilbeck / pixelio.de

More available books at **www.hansebooks.com**

From a Photograph by
Pettigrew and Amos, Leith.

JAMES LUMSDEN.

THE BATTLES

OF

DUNBAR & PRESTONPANS,

AND

OTHER SELECTED POEMS

(NEW AND OLD).

By JAMES LUMSDEN

("SAMUEL MUCKLEBACKIT"),

Late of Nether Hailes, East Lothian,

Author of "Country Chronicles," "Sheep-Head and
Trotters," &c.

HADDINGTON :

WILLIAM SINCLAIR, 63 MARKET STREET.

1 8 9 6.

PREFACE.

—:—

This publication might be described as the poetic portion of my last work—" Sheep-Head and Trotters "—with many omissions and additions ; and it is issued simply because all the former editions are now out of print. With the exception of the new poems, all the others are selected from what now only remains of the whole poetical produce of my life, for I foolishly destroyed the great bulk of it before finally leaving the farm, in a moment of chagrin, worry, and with a feeling akin to despair. The selected pieces—with some others—were saved through having in the course of time been pasted to the leaves of a large private scrap book, and I am quite willing to leave them, with my later offspring, in the hands of all candid readers or critics, stipulating only that they do read the book before pronouncing judgment upon it. The contents of the work have all been carefully revised and are now presented in the best style and guise that I can give them. As I said in my first preface, " I am well aware that the cordial reception most of the pieces met with on their *debut* in their native locality may not prove to have been an earnest of their ultimate success in the world at large. But whatever the fate of this—my latest—literary venture may be, I must now await and accept it with what patience and fortitude I may. I have nothing to advance in the way of anticipating honest, or disarming hostile, criticism. I desire to stand or fall by the merits or de-merits of the book alone." Saving the new poems, "all the pieces contained in the volume were produced in the brief and often interrupted intervals of leisure which the busy life of an arable farmer affords ; and that they have not been permitted to fall into oblivion ere this is no fault of mine, but of my friends, of whom, I am proud to say, I have a large and apparently ever increasing number." God bless them all ! If my gratitude can do them good they will be a happy lot yet indeed !

J. L.

Edinburgh, 1896.

CONTENTS.

—:—

HISTORIC AND LOCAL POEMS.

THE BATTLE OF DUNBAR,

September 3rd, 1650.

—:—

YE Lammermoors, ye silent hills,
  Ye plains an' vales that kythe sae fair !
Thou braid-spread ocean that upfills
  This scene o' peace—beyond compare !

O bide ye in rapt sleep awhile !
  O wake na wi' the morning dawn !
Reck not war's legions thee despoil,
  List not his dread trumps o'er thee blawn !

Alas ! ye happy hills and plains,
  The day breaks that will bring to thee
A heart-break time o' waes an' pains,
  An' mortal mane an' miserie !

Schismatic strife, fanatic zeal,
  Grown furious, meet wi' sword in hand,
Whare priestly arrogance for skill
  Is looten tak' supreme command,—

B

Ev'n while, I trow, the ither side
  Is led by ane—a king o' men !—
What ferly gif the gods decide
  A "glorious victory" he should gain ?

The wauchty Leslie brang them on—
  Twenty an' seeven thousand men —
An' rank'd them on this Hill o' Doon,
  As trig as gin they'd been but ten.

The deep "Lord General" gnaw'd his lip,
  An' claw'd his heid sic skill to dree ;
"The Scot has smat me owre the hip,
  I'm ill at ease, I'm sick !" quo' he.

"For Caldbrand's Pass is closed—nae way
  Is left to back intil Eng-land !—
'Twere best my foot should pack, an' gae
  Tak' ship, an' flee this cursèd strand !

"Syne—grant, O Lord !—I'll head my horse—
  My brethren dear of Marston Moor !—
And burst their ' Pass '—yea—nae—perforce—
  And mak' our swith retreat secure !"

Meantime in either host the " saunts "
  Of countless sects spared not their wind ;
They preach'd an' pray'd, or scream'd their chaunts,
  Or argued ither hairse an' blind.

"This pending battle ? Whey ! the Lord "
  (On this p'int only they agreed)
"The Fae ane harvest for our sword
  Serves ripe an' ready !—shear 't wi' speed !

"Scud doun this hicht!—speare, hack, an' slay!
  Brook not ane Heretick to stand!
All! level all! nane sall gainsay
  Ye Haly Covenant of our Land!

" As Israel ance, at auld Gilgal,
  The Philistines crush'd doun amang,
Sae then do ye! Upo' them fall—
  Ooter destruction mete the gang!"

Sae doun furth this fair hill they sped
  Into the clutch an' pit o' death—
Tumultuous hordes—raw levies—led
  By screichin' clerics—drunk wi' "faith."

O, whare is he, the ae ane man,
  That ever yet could cope wi' "Noll?"
Whare's worthy Leslie wi' his "plan,"
  Anither Bannockburn to poll?

Ah, sirs! he lacked the pith o' Bruce,
  To king-like rule as weel as scheme!
Owre sune the Sophists preach'd him loose,
  Owre sune his rule pass'd like a dream!

Then did the Southrons thank the fools,
  Then did their hearts loup wild to see
The living bands, like weel-play'd bools,
  Row prizes to their feet sae free!

Cromwell out-spak'—he could nae less,
  His very soul cried out for glee—
" Behold! the Lord His cause doth bless,
  He gives His enemies to me!

" Mount ! mount, ye soldiers of the Lord,
    Ye iron-hearted veterans true !
Mount ! fall upon them, pike an' sword,
    They'll be as stubble now to you !"

The onset given by Foot an' Horse,
    What time the risen sun was seen,
Broad in the east, start on his course,
    The combat spread—fast, fierce, an' keen.

Around the hill, down to the sea,
    The war-cluds roll'd, and when they rose
Were seen, high-borne, an' fluttering free,
    The sacred flags o' friends an' foes.

Syne gleams, an' stars, an' flashes white,
    Frae spears, an' swords, an' armourie,
An' brazen guns—glanced, glisten'd bright,
    An' sparkled like the sunny sea.

And wild a' owre ane uproar's heard,
    Like winter storming Norlan' coasts,
And piercing it ilk side's watchword—
    "The Covenant !" and "The Lord of Hosts !"'

And cannon boom'd and muskets crack'd,
    An' swords an' lances clunk between ;
Drums, trumpets, bagpipes, blared an' rack'd,
    An' rived the bleeding Peace in twain !

Then, swith as ye thrice ten micht count,
    The English Horse were victors there ;
Syne up the hill like fiends they mount,
    Wild waving lang swords in the air.

The Scots stude firm—they e'en repulsed
The fore-front foemen, but their best
Were sune cut throo, and then, convulsed
With fear, a' turn'd, an' hamewards prest !

They scatter'd like a hirsel, when
Slee Lowrie-Tod sneaks them amang,
A panic mob—recruits an' men—
A priest-led and sair habbled gang !

In horror Mercy turn'd about,
Forsook the shamefu' scene for good !
Then License, stark-mad, ruled the rout,
And espoused Slaughter—sick with blood !

Yet gloaming cam' at gloaming time,
The harvest moon rose braid an' glad,
But never yet in Scotland's clime
Did e'enin' close owre scene sae sad !

NOTE.—As for other things, the district of Dunbar (one of the most beautiful and interesting in Britain) is celebrated as being the scene of two great national battles, both of which ended disastrously for the arms of Scotland. The first contest took place six centuries ago—on the 28th of April 1296. The cause of this great defeat was an imprudence similar to that which occasioned the one of the second battle, nearly on the same ground, in the time of the Commonwealth. Concerning this now world-famous combat, Robert Chambers says :—" Immediately after the death of the King (Charles I.), when the Cavaliers rose in the North for his son, in what was called ' Pluscardine's Raid,' Leslie sent a party against them in the month of May, 1649, under the command of Charles, Hacket, and Strahan, by whom they were totally dispersed. On the resignation of the Earl of Leven, Leslie was appointed to the chief command of the army raised on behalf of Charles II., after he had accepted the Covenant and been admitted to the Government. In this situation he showed himself an able general, repeatedly baffling by his skill the superior (in discipline and experience, not in numbers) forces of Cromwell, whom he at last shut up at Dunbar, and. but for the folly of the Church and State Committee, which had been the plague of the army during all the previous troubles, had undoubtedly cut off his power.

Red-gasht in bluidy death there lay
Three thousand men, that i' the morn,
In hope and strength sang care awae,
And a' War's dangers laughed to scorn.

*   *   *   *   *

Ye Lammermoors ! ye silent hills !
Ye vales and plains sae sweet and fair !
Thou blue-spread ocean that upfills
This scene o' peace beyond compare !
O hide ye ever in this style,
Wake ne'er again at morning dawn
To see War's legions thee despoil,
Or hear his fiend trumps o'er thee blawn !

Yielding to the importunities of this committee, he rashly descended
from his commanding position, and was signally defeated on the 3rd of
September 1650.   Upwards of three thousand men were left dead on the
field, ten thousand were taken prisoners, two hundred colours, fifteen
thousand stand of arms, with all the baggage and artillery, fell into the
hands of the English.   .   .   .   After the Restoration, Leslie was created,
in consideration of his great services and sufferings in the Royal cause,
Lord Newark, by patent dated the 31st of August 1661, to him and the
heirs male of his body lawfully begotten, with a pension of five hundred
pounds per annum.   .   .   .   His lordship died in the year 1682."

THE BATTLE OF PRESTONPANS.

—:—

" NOW, hail !" cried Cope, "Hail, Prestonpans !
    For saut, for fish, for glorious beer,
The Queen o' touns !—thy creels and cans
    Shall sune this valiant army cheer !

"The morn, my lads, the brek o' day,
    Shall see yon beggary scum doun-dang'd ;
Syne shall the Auld Pans' barrels pay
    Rare price for 'Charlie'—shot or hang'd !

" Great is our drouth—but thole a wee,
    Till ance we've claw'd thae lousy 'clans,'
Then, by this sword ! I vow we'll pree
    A wassail worthy Prestonpans !"

So spak the soople Sir John Cope,
    A cheery captain aye was he ;
His bed that night was Seton slope—
    Him ready graith'd to fecht—or flee !

Athort the Moss, in plaids—or nane —
    The breekless legions of the North,
In raggit herds abreed were lain,
    Like their ain hirsels owre the Forth.

The pawky mune, thro' rifts o' clouds,
    Took merry peeps athwart the plain ;
The wanton winds play'd wi' their duds,
    The caterans snor'd and snor'd again.

Them that had plaids had hapt their chouks,
    An' slept in something decent trim ;
But maist had nane, sae their bare bouks
    Spatted the field baith grue an' grim !

Their watch-fires flicker'd weird alang
    The battle line from east to west,
The silvery Forth lay twined amang
    Her isles an' hills, to silence prest.

Midway atween the muir and sea,
    Like stooks o' beans, the English foe
Spread gross an' dark, the stars on hie
    Spark't as the watch-fires did below.

The careful Cope, behind a tree,
    Gazed sleepless on the clans' array ;
In great surprise an' wrath was he
    They didna rise an' rin awae.

He swat an' steam'd in anxious plicht,
    Aye marvelling they didna flee ;
Till creepin' fogs fill'd all the nicht,
    An' wrapt his sodger's soul in glee.

But sunny morn the misty wraith
    Fast scatter'd wi' the twilicht dun,
Tho' calmness lay on earth like death ;
    Cope fetch'd his horse—he'd heard a gun !

"Hark ! footsteps ; ho, to arms !" he cried,
    "I shall be butcher'd in cold blood !
Up, Gardiner, up ! hast not descried
    The rebel torrent all a-flood ?"

Then thro' the haur belyve was seen
  The clans come on wi' fiery scud,
Each tribe a phalanx, rivalling keen
  Its fellows, wha would first draw blood.

"Upon them, lads!" Clanranald shouts.
  "Cast plaids an' sarks—your bare briests striek ;
Let dirks an' claymores find their throats !
  Strike home ; nor quarter give nor seek."

Then thro' that land the slogans rang
  Wild as thy tempests, Loch-na-Gar ;
Yell rose on yell, while forward sprang
  The mist-born children of Red War.

High in the gloom above the foe,
  Like white sea-birds, the claymores wheel'd ;
And like thae birds they flash'd below
  To a sure prey 'neath Saxon shield.

Oh, dreadful now the battle din !
  As drums an' pibrochs swell'd the fray,
Commingling with the cries of men
  And clank of steel an' musketry.

The twa hosts sway'd in mortal throe ;
  The onset, as a Highland spate,
The English red line—ay or no—
  Met, broke, and o'er-ran in retreat.

One war-like fragment of their wall,
  A while, in god-like majesty,
Stood Christian Gardiner—in his fall
  Made deathless, for he chose to die !

But where was Cope—the sapient Cope—
A prudent Captain aye was he ;
His carcase, friend, on Seton slope
In "cold-blood butcher'd"—seek not ye.

When Charlie charged wi' a' his loons,
Upon his steed the Noble Wicht
Charged in the east the farm touns,
And pat baith sheep and kye to flicht!

Nor dykes, nor yetts, nor collie dougs,
In this invasion he cared nane ;
Frae Hielant clours he saved his lugs,
And Berwick wan—tho' 'twas their ain.

Behind their captain bold, pell-mell,
His faithfu' followers strove an' ran ;
'Tis said they never marched so well
As now, since the campaign began.

In Berwick safe at last, these dregs,
Clawing their cluits like "lousie clans,"
Dree'd that sad nicht—all void the kegs,
And "wassail worthy Prestonpans!"

NOTE.—The far-celebrated Battle of Prestonpans was fought on the 20th of September 1745, just over 150 years ago, between a number of the clansmen of the Scottish Highlands, led by Clanranald in rebellion, purposely to dethrone George the Second, in favour of Prince Charles Edward and his father, and a section of the British army—numbering, horse and foot, about 6000 men—under the command of the illustrious Sir John Cope. The battle, as is well known, issued after the first furious onset of the Highlanders in the complete overthrow and calamitous retreat of the Royalists—and the death of their best soldier, the virtuous and heroic Colonel Gardiner of Preston, whose family mansion stood within gunshot distance of the sad scene of his last moments. A few hours after the brief contest, his body was discovered on the battle-field,

The Highland victors stripped an' reived
Their slaughter'd foemen to the bane :
Boots, sarks, coats, watches were " retrieved "—
Jews pluck gey bare—but they left nane !

---

stripped of everything that had been thought worth carrying away.
Some years ago an obelisk or pyramid monument was erected in his
honour, directly fronting his house at Preston, and close to the main line
of the North British Railway.   As indicated in the ballad, Sir John Cope,
with a few of his followers, hastily sought and found shelter on the
evening of the day of the battle in the garrison town of Berwick—50
miles from "Seton Slope," his dreadful camp-ground of the previous
night.   He arrived none the worse of his long and heroic ride, and slept
well and long.

PUNCH AND DAWTY.

(Two Old Farm Horses.)

—:—

A LOWERING, dour, December sky
Hung o'er the Loudon lands, that lie
Spread out sae braid and bonnilie
Between the Lammermoors and sea ;
Sae green, sae fair in simmer time
They're ca'd the garden o' our clime.

But now they look as drench'd an' droukit
As gif they Noah's flude had sookit—
A' draiglet, dreepin', soddent through
Wi' snawy thows, and jumly broo
Of melted ice, and slush, and rain,
That winter brews and swills amain.

Nae laabor gets the land 'e noo—
It's far owre wat to cairt or ploo ;
The " men" are plouterin' breakin' sticks,
Or in the barn mendin' secks ;
The " cottar bodies" bide at hame,
Whare, eident aye for back and wame,
They bake, or darn and patch their duds,
Or plunge them in the saipy suds ;
And scour and redd a' things sae fine,
Their little housies fairly shine.

Pent cosh within the stable wa's,
The tether'd horses in their sta's
Lounge wearily throughout the day,
Deid tired o' a'—rest, corn, and strae.
Some, drowsy, doze and fitfu' sleep ;
Some, rapt in cogitations deep,
Nod, nod, till in a maze profound
And sage-like, they sleep saft and sound.

The younkers o' the stud meanwhile
Mischievously the hours beguile,
And tak slee nibs at neibors' necks,
Or rive an' pilfer frae their hecks.

But, to speak truth, the ploo naigs maistly
Their dear-prized leisure spen' deuced chastely.
At Clipilaw, as is weel kenn'd,
There's some that for fine manners stand
Conspicuously aboon the heads
Of ither ord'nar quadrupeds ;
And in horse gumption they are great,
And scarcely equall'd ony gate.

Yon farthest aff ane is a meer,
A Clydesdale o'er-gane thirty year,
Fat, sleek, and sonsy, slow—but sure ;
And yet a sicker jaud and dour,
A perfect fiend to turn the sod,
Or birl a cairt, wi' twa ton load ;
A pawky yaad—nor hich nor haughty—
Kent far an' near as " Canny Dawty."

Her neibor in the nearer triviss,
The maist redoubted naig alive is !

For size and strength enormous, famed,
Wham " Punch" his waggish maister named.
Foal'd in the grand year sixty-foure,
Of the royal stock of Staney Tower,
His breed is mixt ; for, in degree,
This was intended, sae that he
Micht shaw the warld, and gar it sing
The glories of its equine king !
For generations his forbears
Were socht for, and were match'd in pairs,
Till, lang an' last, the product was—
This triumph of selection's laws !

He ance had been a model naig,
But noo that character was vague ;
Except for outward form, whilk was
His feature that braucht aye applause.
His image made e'en coupers stare ;
Like a giraffe he tower'd in air ;
His rigid neck was lang and swack ;
The head on 't ae lost e'e did lack.
To fit this philosophic horse,
His frame was baney, huge, and coarse ;
His tail, through some thrawn accident,
Was twisted at the rump asklent,
And hung, as aft I've seen a maud
Hing owre the hurdies o' a jaud,
Belanging to some gipsy scamps,
Stravaigin' on their endless tramps.
His colour, of the hue of fire,
Was weel-toned down wi' muck an' mire.

But this rare stable Patriarch,
Ane-e'e'd, thrawn-rumplet, gaunt, and stark,

Was neither wanting gifts nor grace ;
But in strict fact amang his race
Was for profundity and wits
The Grand Auld Horse elect of bruits.

His efforts oratorical
Proved him nae sorry oracle ;
For, tho' his language was horse Doric,
Their fame micht weel become historic.
A bardie, with the gift of tongues,
Wha's kenn'd for years thae auld ferm bungs,
Has sheaves o' his harangues collated,
And into Scotch them a' translated.
(The *crack* here given best suits our rhyme,
As it took place this vera time !)

PUNCH.

Dear Dawty ! snooze nae mair, my jo !
Our driver, Tam, wha touts thee so,
And aften toobers thee for tricks,
Is at the Big-house sawin' sticks.
He'll no' be back for twa-three hour yet,
Sae crack a wee, my dear, to your mate !

Tell me, Auld Dawt, what's wrang wi' thee,
Why hings thy heid sae pensivlie ?
Why does thy bushy tail sae droop,
Was made thy doup to whisk and soop ?
It micht as weel be in the sea
For ony guid its noo to thee !

DAWTY.

Punch ! weel thou kens an my tail's still,

It's no' because, like thine, it's ill
And feckless, throo a broken rump,
As ony auld wife's toothy stump !
But rather—'care o' me !—because
Of this sair time that on us fa's,
Sairer, and sairer as each year
Comes only but to disappear,
And leave our puir auld maister puirer,
Than wham lives nane mair just or fairer !

It's only three days gane yestreen
Sin' in he papp'd here wi' a frien'
(Upo' the land there was nocht doing,
And thou was at the smiddy shoeing).
Doun on the corn-kist the twa
Held lang converse.   I heard it a' !

Oh, Punch, Punch, Punch ! ane sorrier tale
Did ne'er the lugs o' horse assail !
Its sadness gart me grane an' greet,
And nidder doun to my fowre feet !

The burden of this waesome session
Was " Agricultoorawl Deepression,"
And ither things—owre deep and dark
For sic as me to mind or mark.
They ca'd them " Res-e-pros-e-tee,"
" Keumoolativ Fertilitie,"
" Taxation Incidence ; " and, last,
" Bi-metalism " was up-cast,
And round and round and owre debated,
Till baith the horse and them were sated.

Punch, had ye heard the Maister speak,

'Twad gi'en even thy stiff rump a tweak ;
And e'en thy toom e'e-hole gart blink
And twinge wi' joy—he did *sae* clink
To sense and reason a' the havers,
Whilk are atweel but clishmaclavers !

PUNCH.

But, wumman ! that's nae " *Tale o' Wae !* '
I ken mysel' a' that's to say
About the maitters thou has mention'd ;
And—in thy lug !—I am intention'd
To fall upon and burst thae blethers
.Neist time our Horse Assembly gathers !
But tell me noo, and tell me quickly
What thou o'erheard that made thee sickly.

DAWTY.

O Punch ! wilt thou believe it true ?
The Maister's fail'd !—clean broken throo !
A *broken farmer* and an auld,
To be cuist out o's house an' hald !
And flee—he kensna how or whare,
And find some hole to hatch this care,
And nurse its cleckin' evermair !

PUNCH.

What ! fail'd ! bankrupt ! a dyvour !—HIM !
The Maister bankrupt ? Oh, thou grim,
Black Hag accurst they " Fortune " name !
If aucht on yirth could thee defame
Or bring just evil—now, pell-mell,
Thou'dst flounder fathomless in hell !

C

The Maister fail'd !   Wi' a' my force
I thank my stars I'm but a horse !

DAWTY.

Wheesht ! Punch, man, wheesht ! or sune thy gabble
Shall stir to revolt a' the stable !
The Maister's doun—that tale's owre true,
But 's reason nane for this ado ;
He's doun, and wi' him hunders mair
Already crowd Misfortune's flure !
A giftie crap sure Ruin's threshin'
By " Agricultoorawl Deepression ! "

PUNCH.

Now, Dawty, naething waur can come—
We touch, this nicht, the pit o' Doom ;
And what a change sin' we were 'vaigies,
Twa scamperin', prancin', bits o' staigies,
Wi' snortin' snouts an' flowing tails
Careerin' owre the pasture fiel's,
Wi' twa-three ither cowtes an' fillies,
In summer days—a band o' billies,
And frisky titties—a' as gay,
And fou o' fun as bairns at play !

Nae sough in those days of aggression
By agricultural depression !
Nor were the markets funerals
Of hopes and joys, laid low in shoals !—
But gatherings wi' pleasure fraucht,
Whareat the staff o' life aye braucht
A just and fitting meed to all,
Whase labour, skill, and capital

Had wrung it from the stubborn moor,
And laid it ready at each door !

Faigs ! rent was safe to reckon on
The year that we were broken-in !
(No' "broken" as the Maister 's noo,
But broken-in to cairt and ploo).
It made a differ whan our wheat
Fetch'd three times that whilk noo we geit !
And ither things preportionate—
If no' a tate "extortionate,"
To hantrin folk and burgh bodies,
With wham content a "slavish" mode is !

In such a rowthy, prosperous time,
We and the Maister pass'd our prime ;
And did, safe-like, renew the lease
Of Clipilaw, in hope and peace ;
He little wotting, honest man !—
The *slough o' care* he into ran !—
I saw 't, and spak, but thou forbad' me,
And, sneering, "Jeremiah" ca'd me !

DAWTY.

Yes, Puncher, but thou stand'st sae high,
Nae wonder that thou "sloughs" descry !
At such a hicht, wi' such an e'e,
Thou micht the Bog Sarbonian see !
Thou a True Prophet ! true, I ween,
To prophesee what's *here*, and *seen*.
Gif truly thou this storm foresaw
That now bursts owre auld Clipilaw,
Why did thou ne'er the Maister tell ?

He understands thy neighing well!
But cheep about it, ne'er before
Have I heard thee aince *nicher* owre !

PUNCH.

I daur say no !   How could'st thou hear
A sound that never reach'd thy ear ?
But, saucy hussy ! a' the same,
Know *now*, to thy disgrace and shame
I tauld the Maister years ago
Truly what's come—*to our great woe.*

I tauld him, gin fool folk teuk ferms,
For leases lang, upo' the terms
Whilk me and a' the warld then heard
Were offer'd baith by writ and word,
They wad, as sure as my name's Punch,
On sorrow's soups sune sup and lunch !
Ay ! sup and lunch, and denner, too,
And feast, and feast, and ne'er be fou !

The Maister understood me weel
(For e'en mirac'lous is his skeel
And learning, baith of men and brutes :
He kens us a' frae croon to cloots).
Says he, whan he had heard me out,
" Well, Punch," quoth he, " I hae nae doubt,
" Sid sic things come as thou's observin',
" I wad—my guid auld trusty servan' !—
" Thy Maister *boud*, indeed, cry ' hain ! '
" Gin wheat an' meat frae owre the main
" Cam' in the dreidfu' bulk thy fears,
" For me an' mine in efter years,

" Mak' thee to think an' tell me noo ;
" But, cheer up, auld horse ! and eschew
" Sic dotard fancies !   Thou'rt aware
" ' A faint heart ne'er wan leddy fair ! '—
" The die is cast—the tack's renew'd—
" And, weal or wae, I'se never rued!"
Na, Dawty, he 'se ne'er " rued "—but *yince*,
But *yince* will serve him his life hence,
For it will last his life and him —
Altho' he beat Methoosalem !

DAWTY.

Dear me !   Oh, Punch, what sall we dae ?
We 'se a' be sald, the debts to pay !
I heard him say sae my ainsel'—
Oh, his words rang like my death-knell !—
It 's hard to say owre his narration,
But something he ca'd " Sequestration "
Is cuisten noo owre a' his gear—
Baith deid an' quick—and sair I fear
They'll shaw nae ruth, but in the ring,
At the great sale displenishing,
We 'se a' be run, and have to go
To the best bidder—*ay* or *no !*
Oh dearie me !—that I should dree
Sich 'whalming wae—*and yet no' dee !*

PUNCH.

Sell !   Let them sell us !   Ev'n for *that*
I hae a remedie, dear Dawt !

Sin' we war' brak we've been a pair,
We've ploo'd thegither thirty year !

'For twenty, Tam has been our driver—
A willint fouter, and keen striver ;
Ablins, I micht hae lat *him* slip,
Were he less ready wi' his whip !
But for his leishin's he maun pay—
I'll funk his buttock weel some day !

Dawty, my jo !—tak' tent o' " Punch !"
Gin grief thy breastie rug or runch,
As weel it may, for this last jar
Is a mischance by-ordinar' !

Pruve noo thou art o' noble grit,
And bid despair stand aff a bit !
Mind, naething 's ill but what is thocht ill,
E'en death itsel' to that is brocht still,
By noble and heroic sauls,
Whan high resolve them disenthralls
Frae doited friets and dowie fears—
The weaklin' getts o' waning years !

Gin we maun leave fair Clipilaw
And drag out our auld age, awa'
And far abeigh our native fields,
On mailin's that but slav'ry yields,
Or city streets, mirk-dim wi' smeak,
And dinsome as they 're black and bleak,
Hauling puir cadger muggers' ruchles,
Trockin' auld airn, banes, an' bauchles,
Limping wi' spavie, weeds, an' racks,—
Till at the last, laid on our backs,
Deid, stiff and stark, they hack us sma'
To be by dougs devourit a' !

Sid sic fell fate as this betide us,
What odds, gin Hope stands close beside us,
Her dexter digit pointing free
A heeven for even thou an' me ?
For if such meeds the human class,
Wham we in virtue far surpass,
It stands as plain 's a pheerin' pole—
For brutes there is a sim'iar goal !
O thou condemn'd—this world's accurst !
'Tis writ " the prison bars shall burst—
The first be last—the last be first ! "

There, Dawty, on that happy shore
We 'se meet at last, and part no more !
But wander ever, side by side,
Thro' rowthy pastures, spreading wide,
And greener even than our ain haughs,
Whan spring-time busks the siller saughs !

DAWTY.

The nicht comes slap on efternoon !
The men will a' be here anon !
That thrawn diel Tam wad fell us doun,
Gin he but heard the slichtest soun' !
O Punch—my lord ! my comforter !
I wasna able ev'n to stir,
Or cock a lug, whan thou began !
Noo ! I'm as blythe as whan we ran
Twa playsome foalies wi' our mithers,
And kent o' neither thangs nor tethers !
But Tam 'se be here 'enoo ! May be
Yet at auld Clipilaw we'll dee !
Wha kens but the new Maister man

Will buy us baith, and let us stan'?
Lord grant he may ! my auld heart's set
On this auld place—our auld *hame* yet !
But there they come ! *they 're at the door !*
Oh, govy ! *hoo* that Tam does roar !
We're deid horse, Punch, for wan word more !

ADDRESS TO TRAPRAIN LAW.*

—:—

HAIL! venerable, ample, steadfast friend—
   Dear as a mother's form is thine to me,
So, as a child might, at thy foot I bend,
   To pour this lay of filial love to thee.
Thou wast the wonder of mine infancy,
   And tho' in youth afar I drifted hence,
Again thou art my sacred mount to be—
   Mine own Parnassus—whose high grottoes whence
The mature Muse may sweep the Universe immense !

For thou art as the pivot of my world,
   All round thee circles that I love or know ;
Tho' to the utmost Cosmos Thought were hurl'd
   Back to this source and centre, here below,
Would it rebound—though loathing to forego
   The bootless chase of problems which old Time
Makes mockers of research—life, death and woe—
   The How and Why of Nature's wonders prime—
The secret infinite—the mystery sublime !

To jaded, baffled bard, how calm, how sweet,
   Are thy familiar and mute mountain nooks !
I press thy springy turf beneath my feet,

---

* A striking, and, as seen from the west and north, a high and symmetrical hill, which rises abruptly from the centre of East Lothian to the height of 900 feet above sea level.

I breathe thy purer air—which holds nor brooks
No element to feed the pain that books—
Not Nature's—breed by false imaginings ;
And all my morbid cares take wing, like rooks,
    When sudden March-dawn on their roost-wood
        springs,
And Boreas e'en is hushed with sough of clanging wings.

Then o'er the rounded field of thy grand dome
    And craggy glories of thy southern side,
With zest unwearied do I climb, and roam,
    And revel in the spreading prospect wide,
    Which, from far Ochils to the Northern Tide,
    And from green Lammermoor to Grampians grey
Affords one landscape, seen in summer's pride—
    Might well ev'n Dryasdust himself betray
Beyond his highest flight—lugubrious " Lack-a-day ! "

For what unutterable beauty's given,
    And spread to man o'er this his natal sphere ;
And if this is but earth, what will be heaven,
    Tho' sure its sheen 's anticipated here
    Or its gates stand ajar, and thro' them clear
    A beam celestial streams athwart our strand,
Flooding each valley, moorland, plain, and mere,
    Up to the mountain tips, with mantling grand,
Till rare old Scotia 's dight like an Enchanted Land !

Hither and thither o'er the green expanse,
    Sprinkled with homesteads—as thy slopes   with
        flocks—
Gleaming and glistening in June's radiance,
    The raptured breezes flit in fragrant shocks,

And sing like children 'mong thy rifted rocks
Where I sit musing, blessing heaven the while,
That such a land no malison provokes,
On lawless anarchy, or slav'ry ,vile,
For 'tis of Freedom true the law-ruled home and isle.

Around thy swelling base and beetling crags
No more, Dumpender * ! whirls the rout of war,
Where oft have flouted pitted legion's flags ;
Now the green tree and " milk-white hawthorn " are
Seen waving in this summer peace afar ;
And for the blaring trump and deaf'ning gong,
And shouted slogans of fell foes at jar,
Are heard the low of herds and ploughboy's song,
And that pæon of Art—the railgod's whistle strong !

Ah ! many a change of varying might, I ween,
Hath swept thy ken—alternate rest and throe—
Since thou emerged, nude-born, upon the scene,
Ten thousand times ten thousand years ago !—
Immortal Hill ! the years that man doth know—
A century—fall and effect thee yet
Ev'n less than one light, melting flake of snow
Doth his most lasting hand-work waste and fret,
His vaunted " Pyramids "—Time's laughter and regret !

Before the deluge of the " Flood " had swept
O'er thee the ages as a pall were hung,
'Neath whose dark folds remote thy dead youth slept,
Eras ere Troy was by Homer sung ;
Eras before old Noah was young ;

---

* The old name of Traprain Law.

Eras ere ever from thy flinty grasp
The first rude axe by early man was wrung,
And fashioned with the laborious chip and rasp,
In search of food or foe—his trusty friend to clasp.

And as thy semblance now, so in past time,
Thou must have look'd and filled that concave sky,
Bending all round thee its old arch sublime—
Summer's and winter's one fit canopy !
With all thy brethren round thee far and nigh—
Edina's Crags, Inchkeith, sea-level May,
Bass, Berwick, Doon Hill, and the Lammer high ;
Gullane and Garleton, and—far away—
Old Scotia's cloud-like seats—the " Bens " and Grampians
grey.

Thus ever 'midst our Lothian garden set
Uprear thy cairn-top'd cupola for aye :
Colossal dome ! no nakedness regret !—
Thy massive splendour needs no trickery gay !
A mountain and a monitor alway,
As palpable to dullest thought as sight ;
Teach thou the hordes of men that fleet away
The lesson of thy time-enduring might—
Thy pledge of glorious hope—to those who read aright.

THE LEGEND OF TRAPRAIN LAW.*

—:—

KING LOTH, the Grim, sat on his throne —
Owre a' the Lothians King was he ;
Nor friend nor kin loved he, but ane—
Ismolde—his ae fair daughter, she.

To castled Hailes his warriors beat—
Thanes and wise men, frae far and near
In troops, on horse, or sandal'd feet,
With flowing locks and warlike gear.

---

* " King Loth, who held sway in the Lothians, and to whom the county
is indebted for its name, had a fair and only daughter, on whose brow the
diadem was in due time to repose. The monarch kept court at some
quarter of his dominions not far from Traprain. A shepherd youth lived
at this place, with whom the young princess fell hopelessly in love.
Stolen interviews followed, and the king too late discovered that his
daughter had brought disgrace on her lineage. The punishment was
death, and that in one of the most appalling forms. The erring damsel
was taken to the top of Traprain, and was thrown from the dizzy height
of three or four hundred feet to the plain below. The spot where she
fell was ever afterwards known by a spring of delicious water that burst
forth from the ground the moment she alighted upon it. She was found
by her friends not quite dead, but insensible, and was conveyed t) the
shores of the Forth, where she was put in an open boat, and left to drift
at the mercy of the tide. The wind and waves proved more merciful than
her unforgiving sire, and the still unconscious but miraculously preserved
lady was wafted in her frail bark as far as Culross, where she gave birth
to a son, who, under the name of St Mungo, became the patron saint of
Glasgow. One day, not far from the spot where his daughter had fallen,
King Loth was espied and killed by the peasant lover. He was buried at
the base of the hill, and, according to the chronicler who relates the story,
a stone was raised to tell future generations where he had been laid."—
D. CROAL.

And dern they bear their Saxon brands—
    Sword, dagger, spear, and battle-axe ;
While swings the mace, with iron bands
    Clampt like Thor's hammer, at their backs.

Athort the fosse they jostle in—
    Thane, Viking, Scald, and Odin's priest—
And fill the Hall with clam'rous din,
    As 'twere to jocund wassail feast.

But wherefore sits the King so pale,
    In sable, throned on wool-pack hie ?—
Before that throne arraign'd is one,
    Now doom'd for death, Ismolde is she !

" Daughter of Kings ! thy weird betide,
    I Loth, Bretwalda, Lord, and King,
From Eastern Merse to Strath of Clyde,
    Thy Prince, in judgment, 'gainst thee bring.

" By right and birth this seat were thine,
    By deadly sin now lost ere won !
Alack the day ! that child of mine
    So base could stoop to born thrall's son !

" Yea ! not to stoop, but seal with love,
    Before the gods, thy royal troth !
Dread Thor ! Valhalla's gates above
    Burst vengeance full for childless Loth !

" Yon smooth Oswald of Deira, he
    That, homeward bound from Columb's isle,
Foot-sore, sojourn'd a space with thee,
    Hath fool'd thy head with tales the while.'

" Oh, father ! " cried the noble maid,
" Oh, royal Loth, traduce him none !
Ralph loved me since we children played ;
    I love him for his worth alone !

" Who mated me from earliest days ?
    Who shamed Fife's champion bow and spear ?
Who saved *thee* from the dreadful assays
    Of wild Scots on the Ochils drear ?

" Deny him not ! but Ralph I love.
    Or weal or woe—I care not else !
As for the gods—One reigns above ;
    Our fathers' gods, as dreams, were false ! "

" Say'st thou ? Those gods confound the wench,
    And by their god-given power in me,
Their wrongs and mine this night I'll quench
    In thy heart's blood—mine tho' it be !

" Lost child of Hengist ! list thy weird :
    From Traitor's Rock, Dumpender Hill,
Be thou cast forth this eve—declared
    Ill traitress, ripe for death as ill !

" And let thy bones unhousen'd rot—
    Fit carrion for the night boar now !
Accursed whereon they fall the spot,
    Grim haunt of gorgons—curst as thou !

" And torn from mouth of him the tongue
    That henceforth names thy name shall be !
And death his guerdon—old or young—
    Who this black day wouldst succour thee ! '

So spoke the tyrant, and withdrew ;
  Him none in all that Hall gainsaid ;
Forth rushed his murd'rous menial crew,
  And as 'twere wild beast, bound the maid !

They've ta'en her to that dreadfu' Hill ;
  No plaint made she, no word she spake,
But whiter than her white robe still,
  Her ghastly face your heart might break.

They stand upon the fatal rock—
  How hush'd that star-lit gloaming's pause !
They from her limbs the thongs unlock—
  How hushed sad eve night's curtain draws !

O, they were twenty stalwart men,
  She but a maiden slim and slight ;
Thus high in arms, Ismolde is ta'en,
  And flung sheer forth that awful height !

As white downpours a mountain flood
  O'er crag and cliff upon the heath,
As drops an eagle from the cloud,
  Whom fowler's barb has carried death,

So fluttering fell the fair Ismolde—
  That vicious thrust the Saxons gave
From scarps and jagged peaks untold
  Her fragile form unscath'd did save.

Their brute strength proved her boon, I trow ;
  Their Saxon lack of ruth her gain ;
O, for her lover champion now,
  With arms outstretched upon the plain !

Alas ! 'twas but a birken tree—
  Ralph, far in Fife, Loth's ire had flown —
But blessings on that birken tree
  And the soft sward she lights upon !

Sae dreid her fate, sae pure her heart,
  Her safety gart the breezes sing,
And frae the ground she landed on
  Flows welling aye a caller spring.

Close on the witching hour o' night,
  Stowlins, old Madge, her nurse, drew near,
And swarf'd outright wi' gladsome fright,
  Yet moaning low, Ismolde to hear !

Like wearied babe she lifted her ;
  Like nurse gane gyte, away she fled,
Nor baited she till o'er the sea,
  Ismolde in fisher's skiff she'd sped.

The Powers aboon look friendly doun,
  Nor nigh that bark came storm nor strife !
It drifts anon by Culross toun—
  Stronghold of Oscar, King of Fife.

The King held Beltane on the strand,
  " What drifting wrack is yon ? " cried he ;
" Come, Claude, Harewolf, and Louden Ralph,
  Who takes it first—*his* prize shall't be !

Three galliots, like three proud swans,
  That sweet May morn shot o'er the sea ;
And oars were plied like willow wan's—
  But Ralph right nobly bore the gree.

D

"A hooly prize, fair won, my lad !
   A hooly prize !" the King cried he ;
"Hist thee ashore the foundling moor—
   What ocean stray-waif mot she be ? "

Moor'd high and dry, they round it pry,
   "Jesu ! " cried Oscar, " what is here ?"
As from the hold the fair Ismolde,
   From deep sleep waking, 'gan to peer !

Dumfoundered—ghaistlier than ghaist,
   And staggering as a champion fell'd—
"O King ! " cried Ralph, " be this no jest—
   A miracle is here beheld !

"This is the maid, for whom I said,
   I'd flown her pagan father's ire !
Fair won, Ismolde, let me unfold
   A ' hooly prize,' indeed, my Sire ! "

Oh, Oscar was a knightly King—
   A Beltane wedding gave he both ;
But when Ismolde her tale had told,
   His vow he pledged to chastise Loth.

When Hallowmas had swept the plain,
   A fleet of ships stood o'er the Forth—
Oscar's bold eagle, freed again,
   In full broad light from furth the North.

But Oscar was the truest knight,
   And in surprise did scorn to take
Even Loth ; quo' he—" We come to fight,
   Not slaughter, ev'n for Ismolde's sake.

"Speed, envoy, then, to Court of Loth,
    Say—' To redress foul murder home,
A thousand gallants, bound by oak,
    Even Oscar and his knights have come.'

" The deed he knows—but give this ring,
    Rasped from the nape of Ralph—a thrall,
Who wed the fallen child of his King,
    Yet nathless comes to 'venge her *fall !*"

To Castled Hailes the envoy came,
    And told King Oscar's challenge full ;
King Loth—no warrior lag or lame—
    Full wroth, his royal beard 'gan pull.

" Back, braggart, back to Seton's Bent ;
    Let all your Highland stags be shown ;
Thy heid's a feast by Odin sent
    Our Saxon dogs to gorge upon ! "

Around Dumpender's western base,
    Upon them Oscar's knights did fall,
And many a rueful Saxon face
    That day kiss'd mother earth withal.

Wild was the fray—like boars at bay
    The Saxons fought frae dawn till dine ;
And blude eneuch by mony a sheugh,
    Gart lang or night rin red the Tyne.

When Oscar charged the tyrant Loth,
    Their spears both in flinders flew ;
Syne swacked they swords in deidly wroth,
    But a churl behind King Oscar slew !

The sacred spot the hero fell
  Tells to this day his Standing-Stane ;
Another, nearer to the Hill,
  Where Loth by Ralph was fought and slain !

AULD HANSEL MONDAY.*

—:—

WHAN grim King Winter hauds his reign
'Mang trains o' gloom appearin',
Auld Hansel Monday comes again
Wi' routhy mirth an' cheerin';
His look is like the Freend o' Man's—
To auld and young endearin';
A haill year's walth is in his han's—
He scatters without fearin'
To a' this day !

His bags are fou o' wondrous cheer,
His social face is glowin'

---

* Hansel Monday, the first Monday of the new year, is equivalent
to Boxing Day in England and America. Auld Hansel Monday is the
first Monday after the 12th of January, the New Year's Day in old style.
Both days have the same signification. Auld Hansel Monday originated
at the time of the Reformation. There were certain well defined and
marked holidays and festival seasons, and Christmas, or Yule, was the
chief one. At this period, in feudal times, it was customary for the lord
of the manor to present his retainers with a " box," or gift, hence Boxing
Day. After the overthrow of the Papacy the stern Presbyterian divines
proved themselves so zealous for the cause of the new faith that they even
forbade their flocks to observe the old holidays. Christmas, it was given
out in every pulpit in the land, was to be obliterated at once. Every
good man, and every matron and maiden, was commanded to be at the
plough, or to bring the spinning wheel and work at it before the eyes of
all men at the cottage door on that day—defaulters to sit on the creepie
stool for three consecutive Sundays. The very huskings of Popery were
to be burned up and not a visible shred to remain. In pity, however, those
ardent theological reformers, for the loss of the old Yule, humanely
granted their devoted followers a gift, or hansel day, which they appointed
should be the first Monday of the year, old style. In Banff, Fife, Peebles,
and other parts, Hansel Monday—the first Monday of the year—is still in

Wi' heartfelt glee—tho' whiles a tear
Doun his fat cheek is rowin' ;
On happy auld lang syne thinks he !
But shortly does it tout him,
For auld Scots hospitality
Mak's a'thing round about him
    Blythe, blythe this day !

Hail, merry morn ! the puir man's day !
When furth the cottar's fowre wa's
Care packs him aff without delay
To girn in touns his puir cause !
Then ilka en', Jock's butt and ben,
The lichtsome foot on floor fa's,
O' rustic joy, nor shy nor coy
When Time a fittin' hour shaws,
    As now this day.

By screich o' morn the bairns are up,
And loud the auld folk rousin' ;

---

a fashion observed, but it is only in East Lothian, and in a part of East
Lothian only, that Auld Hansel Monday is recognised and observed in
anything like its pristine glory. It is there a hallowed name to East
Lothian men, women, and children. Auld Hansel Monday ! With it are
associated feelings, and thoughts, and fond longings and yearnings of the
human heart peculiarly. With it are associated the tenderest memories
of the family and the fireside circle, and every home tie that a loving
heart holds dear. From the loud-sounding, sense-confounding, and busy
cities come the servant girls, the shop boys, and the artisans, back to their
native calf-ground. Whole families are re-united, with here and there,
alas ! a friend amissing. In the rapid glance of the eye, in the
hurried, vigorous grasp of the hand, untold volumes of well-understood
meanings are conveyed by Scottish men and women from one to another
on Hansel Monday morning. Long-suppressed feelings have this day an
outlet. The village streets, from an early hour in the morning, are
thronged with visitors. The early trains bring in large numbers of them
from every quarter. From the surrounding rural districts come all the
forenoon literally crowds of youngsters, well-dressed, respectable-looking
young men and "bonnie lasses," and grave, sagacious-looking, con-
scientious, grey-headed Scotchmen—men, the like of whom can be seen
in no other country.

What braws are donn'd, what sangs are conn'd,
　　What daffin' an' carousin'!
The parritch pat this morn I wat,
　　The mice themsel's may doze in—
On rarer fare baith rich an' puir
　　Do deeply shute their nose in
　　　　Wi' joy this day!

Our wames appeas'd, the young an' stout
　　Maun graith them for the shootin';
And mony a queer gun's faitchin' out,
　　And bullets ticht to put in.
Tam shouthers ane like a rain spout—
　　A roostit Copenhagen,
That "even Auld Nick wi' couldna shute,"
　　As Pate confides the lug in
　　　　O' Jean this day!

Aff wi' the lads—we leave a while
　　The auld folk, bairns, and lasses,
Wha cosh at hame, shall time beguile
　　Wi' ane and a' that passes;
Sae brisk and bauld we jump the stile,
　　And for the toun address us,
Owre wintry roads, for mony a mile
　　Thick-thrang wi' maist a' classes,
　　　　Gaun lowse this day!

The toun it stands beside a burn
　　That loups a rockie linn there,
And as below the brig we turn—
　　Oh, Wow! the deavin' din there!
The Linn, galore, did ramp an' roar,
　　And trains an' crowds cam' in there;

And whalm'd an' whirl'd, and brawl'd an' birl'd,
    And vortex-like did spin there,
        This awfu' day !

The " Red Lion's " fount our drouth maun slake
    Wi' genial Jamie's best ane,
Syne to the Games, weel-primed, we'll make,
    And see the grand contestin' !
Within a ring o' hemp an' stake,
    Some chields their claes are castin',
While shifting crowds around them break
    In laughter loud an' jestin',
        Richt gleg this day !

In skin-ticht duds o' flannel soy,
    They loup, and rin the races ;
Lang, lang they've practised for this ploy,
    Noo they maun shaw their paces.
But vain, alas !   Baith man and boy
    The day ere lang disgraces ;
Few win, maist fa' and sair destroy
    Their braws, or splairge their faces
        Wi' glaur this day.

Hammers and cumbrous caubers now
    Like willow wands they're swingin' ;
Wi' wild huzzas at each big throw
    The startled lift is ringin' ;
But we maun go—the targets, ho !—
    And leave the giants flingin'
Their shafts an' dread bolts to and fro,
    Like Jove, some great god bringin'
        To grief this day !

"Three shots a shillin'!—bleeze awa';"
A sturdy auld carle cries us,
As we draw near the butts in fear
O' burstin' guns' surprises;
"A muckle cheese, twa chairs and a',
Forbye some tea, 's the prizes,
Ma faith! he is nae man ava
Wha comes an' never tries us
Ae round this day!"

Dick shouthers first the trusty gun
That craw-herd Johnnie lent him
(Wha chuckie stanes wi't, mony a pun',
Amang the sprugs had sent 'em),
He took a lang and deadly aim
At the bull's e'e fornent him,
Syne steekt his een, an' fired as game
As gin his lass ahint him
Look'd on this day.

Whare did the wayart bullet speed?
Gae speer in Beanston Valley;
The muckle target, right a-heid,
It cleared as clean 's a swallow!
Tam neist for Copenhagen paid
His last bob—but, puir fallow,
Not even a lowin' clout to 't laid
Could coax a single volley
Frae it this day!

Lang, lang, wi' friendly joke an' crack
The crowd gart muskets smack there,
But gif the target ere ane strack
We didna stey to mak' sure.

On leaving, as we keekit back,
  All huge in white and black there,
It stude, defying the haill pack,
  As lairge, and as intack there,
    As Sol this day.

Sune ran we hame wi' anxious haste
  For our grand Hansel denner,
Pork chops and dumplins, sic a feast,
  A boon for saunt or sinner.
Our country core were a' weel braced,
  And wearyin' to begin her ;
The board's richt eithly served an' graced
  That's spread for health-an' hunger
    Like ours this day !

The furious onslaucht, knife and fork,
  Was a' owre in a whuffy,
Sae weel our tusks an' talons work
  In this wee glorious jiffy.
At Prestonpans his Hielant dirk
  Nae clansman plied mair stuffy,
Than did our lads their weapons yerk
  Amang the creesh an' taffy,
    In lochs this day.

And aye atween the stechs, galore,
  We pree the tither drappie,
To synde the gusty mouthfu's owre
  And clear our claggit crappy ;
Ilk lad and lass their glasses pass,
  And touzzle owre the nappy ;
The auld folk see, but let a-bee,
  And wyte the time sae happy
    For pranks this day.

When toasts were dune and things aside,
  In stumps auld Andrew Brodie,
Wha in his oxter, like a bride,
  His fiddle braucht, blythe body ;
He screwed her up wi' conscious pride,
  And rosin'd her that snoddy,
He saw'd us aff sweet Kelvinside, ·
  Like Gow, inspired wi' toddy
    And sneesh this day.

Then soon wi' reels, and " waltzes," even,
  The wee cot housie dirled,
As a' the blasts o' yearth an' heaven
  Were 'gainst its boukie hurled ;
Braw lads and lasses lap and skirled,
  Bang men, and folk wha'd striven
Man's number'd years in this hard world,
  Cried " heuch ! " like warlocks driven
    Clean gyte this day.

But daffin', jigs, an' sangs, an' tales,
  Sped far too swith the hours on,
For freends were met whom morrow's gales
  Must waft apart life's course on.
Anither year, and maybe ne'er
  Again while time's flood roars on,
Might they e'er meet, or even greet,
  Abune this world's horizon,
    Tho' here this day !

Weird hopes and fancies fill'd each heart,
  A wild fond sadness moved us ;
We lingered lang—sae laith to pairt,
  And the " farewell," it proved us !

But blessings on that Hansel ploy,
    It aye the mair behoved us,
To pray the Powers—for oh, what joy
    It braucht wi' those wha loved us,
        This matchless day !

HOGMANAY.*

---:—

ET sighing " saunts " and mim-mou'd bards
   Rant owre their " dying year ;"
The rustic muse, mair meet, awards
   And speeds 't wi' sang an' cheer,
And joys that Mirth, as far owre earth
   As common sense hath sway,
'Mang simple folk her e'e shall cock,
   And welcome Hogmanay
      Ance mair this nicht.

Auld Hogmanay ! The funniest nicht,
   Tho' hindmost o' the year ;
Thou ev'n in sulkiest, sourest wicht
   Gars gleams o' glee appear ;
And young an' auld mak' blythe an' bauld,
   And nane but sumphs look glum,
Whan cakes and ale a'where prevail
   Till dyvours even are rum
      Wi' joy this nicht !

---

* New Year's Day Eve. The customs and practices described in the
above verses were universally in fashion amongst the peasantry of East
Lothian in the writer's early days. Nor are they altogether forgotten or
obselete yet in the rural parts of the country. The "big bands" of
mummers or guisers, indeed, may not be as often met with now as
formerly, but this time-honoured species of frolic is still very common
and popular amongst the country and village children during " Yule
Tide "—and especially on the evening of Hogmanay.

The youngsters in yon wee cot hoose
    At hame whare we were born,
This nicht, task-free, are looten lowse,
    And merry guisers turn :
Fause-faces on, and sarks they don
    Abune their coats an' breeks ;
Syne ramp an' roar frae door to door,
    And tirl the neebors' snecks
            Like ouphes this nicht !

Against this time, for weeks before,
    They've conn'd their plays and sangs :
Sae furth they troop, equipped galore,
    In noisy gleesome " gangs."
And ilk guidman and wife affhaun'
    The " bairns " richt welcome gi'e,
For lang, lang syne they bring to min',
    Whan they themsel's wad be
            " Guisers " this nicht !

Whyles Kate or Johnny's feart an' blate,
    But ane—their " Judas " he—
Is, sure, nae " Muff " at onyrate,
    Tho' timmer tuned he be.
Sae furth he stands, and shouts wi' pride—
    " Goloshan is my name !
With sword and pistol by my side,
    It 's *me* shall win the game,
            Ye dwarfs, this nicht !"

Whereat a mannikin wee " lord "—
    A kid Napoleon—
Strides out, and waves his wooden sword,
    Crying, " Golosh, follow on !

The game, sir ! the game, sir !
  It 's not within thy pow'r,
For with this—my bloody dagger—
  I shall flay thee on that floor,
        Thou sheep, this nicht !"

Like Celts at feud they weapons wiel',
  But little Nap, I trew ;
Like Nap the Great, sin pruves his skill,
  And rins his foeman " through."
Then giant *Golosh* on the floor,
  A driedfu' doom wad dree,
But " Doctor Gore " does him restore,
  As soond as you or me,
        Wi' a *funk* this nicht.

Lang ere the tragedy is closed,
  A' bashfulness hath fled ;
Ilk youngster's lilt will sune be lowsed,
  And bawbee ballads said ;
Syne currant scones, and ha'p'nies round,
  Will mak' their hogmanay ;
And merrier weans may not be found
  In Christendie than they,
        This joyous nicht.

But noo, in yonder auld toom hoose,
  A greater band convene—
Big country chiels, an' cummers crouse,
  And halflin' lads a wheen ;
Out-workers, they, their toggery gay,
  The lads wi' lasses swap ;
And as ilk ane, transformed comes in,
  Wi' mirth they maist do drap,
        Like drunks this nicht.

Jock Skaed in Maggie Ritchie's goun,
    And dress-improver lairge,
Comes airm in airm wi' wild Tam Broun,
    Wha, despite cost or chairge,
Is buskit out, and flounced about—
    For a' his tawny baird—
Like Royal Bess in a "progress,"
    When wi' Leicester's laird
        She toy'd at nicht.

Wee Katie Todd, sae sweet an' snod,
    For a' her toils obscure,
Comes thundering in wi' Kirsty Glen,
    A brigand blackamoor ;
And Jeanie Hogg, the winsome rogue,
    And rage o' a' the toun,
Ev'n joins the band—togged like a grand
    And dashing smart dragoon,
        Love-bound this nicht !

Whan they've a' met, the band will tell,
    Wi' fiddlin' Joseph More,
And Hielant piper, Rob M'Call,
    Both sexes—near a score ;
And, for time's short, they tak' the road,
    Belyve wi' richt guid will ;
The mune comes oot in heaven abroad,
    And glamourie rare will fill
        The warld this nicht.

The starrie gleans thro' rifts an' seams
    Of stormy skies are seen,
And darklin' wuds, like thunder cluds,
    Tower huge and black between

The shadowy fields, and ourie bields,
    Whare lonesome flocks repose ;
The winds sough by, and seem to sigh-—
    "The Auld Year's at a close,
            And dees this nicht !"

The guiser bands meet guiser bands,
    And merrily fraternise ;
Their lood guffaws, like storms on strands,
    Resound alang the skies,
And echo frae the wondering hills,
    As freends at kenn'd freends start ;
In sooth their looks micht scare life's ills
    Frae even an auld maid's heart,
            Love-lorn this nicht.

Anon they pairt in hurrying glee,
    And rin their several ways,
For lang the tramps this nicht do be
    That ilka band essays ;
Our gentry's ha's for miles around,
    Maun stage their mimic fun,
And ilk ferm house 'ithin their bound
    Be in its turn owre-run,
            Ere twal this nicht.

Their pipes an' fiddles skirl an' squeck,
    And, on the flaggit floors,
They dance till doors and winnocks shake,
    And own the plough-boy's pow'rs ;
And gentles draw in Grange an' Ha'
    To swithly join their plays—
A' folk are loved—a' hearts are moved,
    And melt in Hogmanay's
            Warm clasp this nicht !

The yill gaes round—sangs, toasts abound,
    Wow ! hoo the gentles laugh !
Our proud Queen Bess, in his Court dress,
    Ev'n condescends to quaff
A flowing can " To the gudeman
    And mistress o' this house ; "
Wha, pleased, rejoin, and a gowd coin
    Slip him, for the band's use
        And treat this nicht.

Meantime the auld folk, blythe at hame,
    Await the youths' return,
Wi' neebors they a winning game
    Play wi' John Barleycorn :
Auld yarns are spun, auld ballads sung—
    Screeds heard but ance a year ;
The spell-bound bairns—baith auld and young—
    Sit up, them a' to hear
        Again this nicht !

But anxious keeks are gi'en the clock—
    Nae mean Wag-at-the-Wa',
But ane frae Alec Cameron's stock,
    An " aucht-day," lairge and braw—
Its twa hands maist meet at the twal,
    When, sudden at the door,
The band, returned, are heard to brawl,
    And gabble owre their store
        O' gifts this nicht.

Fu' sune they crood the cottar's house,
    Till guests and guisers fill
Its butt and ben sae fou, a mouse
    A cat there couldna kill.

And they a' stare the aucht-day clock,
 And every saul is dumb—
Husht—listening for the Auld Year's stroke,
 And the—" I come ?   I come !
Lo ! I am here, the New-born Year,
 On the ' for ever ' cast ;
To strive and speed, thro' peace and feide,
 Till I shall gasp my last,
   Twal months this nicht."

The haill crowd bound upo' their feet,
 And, with a Scotch huzza,
They joyously the New Year greet,
 And shake hands ane an' a'.
The young chaps bring their bottles out,
 And ilk ane gets a wettin' ;
Syne, sune's they've tasted, turn about,
 They a' set aff first-fittin'
   On New Year's morn !

THE HIRING FRIDAY.*

—:—

AS business call'd, I gaed to toun,
    An' braved the hiring warsle ;
So thae " impressions " I note doun
    O' the great human hirsel.
Morosely, by a glowing fire,
    I retrospect the habble :
Yet scorn my soon-suppressed desire
    To execrate the " rabble."

For while humanity is dust,
    And man a vagrant creatur'—
Whase aft daft antics bring disgust
    Your " sagely " meditator ;
He is not all he seems to be
    In holiday careering ;
Aft thro' the scum of foamy sea,
    The pearly treasure's peering.

Where ignorance and folly meet
    Wi' youthfu' glee to prompt them,
What if vulgarity should greet,
    An' her dear children compt them ?
The boorish speech, the gait, the leer,
    An' mind a blank—we pity,

---

* This is a "red-letter" day in the lives of the peasantry of East
Lothian—the Hiring Friday at Haddington.

Yet what ye lack—God's truth—is here,
  Ye shams in toun or city !

Here simple human nature shaws,
  All unsophisticated ;
Unknown, unheeding fashion's laws—
  Her yearning heart unsated !
That one heart, worn on rustic sleeves
  This day for knaves to peck at
Is Adam's still—and joys and grieves
  Or plush or purple deck it.

Still, cross'd was I our manlike "hinds "
  To see them fool'd an' cheat'd,
By gallows scamps, wi' tricks an' blinds,
  A school miss might defeated !
By riff-raff rogues, whase victims were,
  In a' that decks the wearer,
To such tag knaves—as Tyneside air
  To Cowgate reek—superior !

But drunts aside ; the " ither facts,"
  Let us a moment scan them—
Behold auld Scotland's buirdly backs,
  An' shanks *that shaw men awn them !*
" Beloved at hame—revered abroad ! "
  The " wall of fire " around her !
The arm with whilk she cuts her road
  When thick faes would confound her !

An' lasses, sweet ! as lads are stoure !—
  Braw cockernonied ladies !
Show faces that would papists sour,
  Mak' benedicts an daddies !

Nae prim-faced, dwarfish, dolly jades
That cankered guidmen bothers,
But, "plump an' strappin'" stately maids—
Proud Scotland's future mothers !

ROBERT BURNS.

[WRITTEN ON AN ANNIVERSARY OF HIS BIRTH,
IN MY EARLY DAYS.]

—·:—

OH, Muse of Caledon ! with fervid wing
    From the blue hills thou mak'st thy sacred seat,
With mountain cataract and cliff interned,
To our stream'd valley in a strath lowland
Descend !' and justly of thy minstrel true,
This day—his day—to us the day of days,
Commemorative of him evermore,
Teach me, child-like, to sing !   O'er heirs of fame
Of ours above—philosophers, or they
Whose martial story or historic page
Or song confounds decay—his laurel'd head,
Spiring the groups of Scotia's giant sons,
Towers like a king's.   No longer moody brow'd,
I see him o'er his empire sweep his eye—
The master of the fields of song beloved,
Sowing and reaping joy !   No truer eye
E'er peep'd, like lover, into Nature's face
So sympathetic with the love of her—
He grew unto her, and her breath was his,
His, hers—them both a melody,
Wedding their two souls—one !
                    "Sweet Ballochmyle !"
The dew-eyed spirit of a summer's eve,
Tender and loving as the face of pity,
In one small song !

Then, as we turn the page,
And reading—" Scots wha hae wi' Wallace bled ! "
A blast, as of Mar's thunder, wakes the heart,
And the most peace-wed souls, with sudden fire,
Blaze with heroic ire and martial eye
As patriots arm'd ! "Should Auld Acquaintance
Be forgot ?" Never ! Thou hast made it sure
It never can ! That query is a spell
To sprite the querist's name from age to age—
To the fag end of time ; and being there,
To charm time back again. Turn me the leaves :
Not one of which but glows with Nature's light
As sweet as sweet eves, when the harvest moon
Keeps watch the golden field, and overhead
The plover's cry is heard ! Here's an old friend—
" A man's a man for a' that ! " So he is—
But many a man was scarce a man before
Ye breach'd his mind and let the knowledge in
That makes him so. Given assurance true
Of the grand fact—a man he surely was—
He one became ; mayhap a slave before,
Or cringing yokel to exacting "lord ; "
With cap in hand, and fearful downcast eye,
Mumbling the enforced homage abjectly,
His soul as darksome as his gait confess'd,
The immortal mandate—" A man's a man,
The rank is but the guinea stamp, the man's
The gowd for a' that !"—charged as with Heaven's fire,
Lit up his darkness, as the levin bolt
Night's murky gulf, and let him see the ground
Whereon they both stood was the equal earth—
The earth, nor less, nor more !
                Henceforth, to both

All life was changed ;—the lordling doffed his pride,
Forgot his "strut ; " the serf, a serf no more !
Shoulder to shoulder stood up with the port
And modest dignity that graces man,—
The bluest princeling's peer !
                    But to resume :
"Highland Mary ! " " Ye Banks an' Braes ! " "Tam
        Glen ! "
Each one of these, and eke a hundred more—
All matchless—Scotia doth hold dear, and sings
Them to all peoples of the wondering lands,
Who drink their rapture from her dulcet lips
With charmed and greedy ears, till they, entranced,
Grow dead to every care of all the world
But her harmonious woe !
                    In many a clime,
In many a land of many-corner'd earth,
In Indian jungles and Columbian wastes,
In Afric arids and mysterious wilds,
Islands, like Edens, in the purple seas,
Pacific, and Australian worlds,
The wondrous opposites and heirs of ours,
As well King Winter's realms—the home of Frost—
Hudson's and Lapland—these old songs of Burns,—
Like veriest wizards in the human heart,
Have conjured with the weary exile's thoughts,
And in the sighs of longing wanderers,
Bewitched impossibles to patent facts ;
And o'er the *frem* and foreign continents
Made misty Scotland with her hills arise
To fondest memory true !
                    There is a gem—
A talisman in two brief verses—which,

Many a dreary hour in Far West lands—
Hath, like a mother's voice, soothed me to peace,
And pillowed in the awesome wilderness,
My home-sick troubled heart, and made me love,
Like hers, the name of Burns !
The Poems now.—To me—to every Scot
Whose unsophisticated breast is proof
To ward aside the testy showers of cant,
Like April rain,—these Scottish poems are
("Familiar in our mouths as household words ")
Sources of richest, never-ceasing joys ;—
Fountains of never-failing glorious mirth,
With humour spurting to the gravest verge !—
Repositories rare of Fancy's spoils,
Which she, when raiding with her Scottish Knight,
Carried from Dreamland's territories bright,
Where Beauty, absolute, sits Queen of Art
And universal song.   Here we behold
Fruit mellow as the tree whereon it grew ;
Angelic tenderness and satire keen ;
Piercing sagacity and wisdom sage ;
A sword of wit, with which this David slew
The Giants—humbug and hypocrisy !
A laverock-throated bird of sentiment,
That, singing, makes our hodden-grey Scotch sky
Beyond the radius of semi-earth,
Glint with the harmonics of inspired thought
And raptured feeling—as the glamoury dome
Of Poesy's own Fane !
                    And here we meet—
Description in her simple robes of truth,
Sweet nurse and ruler of the Poet's art,
Leading in either hand, through all his works,

The seen and the ideal—sisters twain—
Up to perfection's feet.   For all do feel,
Who read both Nature's and the poet's book —
The fact that Nature cannot clearer prove
That she is Nature, than the page of Burns,
Her faithful bard, attests !   Graved with his pen,
Her happy lineaments pluck from our eyes
Amazed conviction, with the infant view
Which recognises them !

AT PRESTONKIRK.

[MARCH 12TH, 1888.*]

—:—

THE eastlin' wind blew cauld an' keen,
  The auld Kirkyaird was clad in snaw,
But eastlin' wind or snaw, I ween,
  That day I neither felt nor saw.

My heart was in a coffin there,
  Slow sinking down an open grave ;
The wide world micht be foul or fair
  For me, sae sunk in sorrow's wave.

I kenn'd the king that coffin held,
  As nane on earth could ken like me,
An' loyal love would not be quelled,
  An' death but quickened memorie.

My thochts, like birds, winged thro' the past,
  Dead summers blossom'd green again ;
I saw that king, baith firm an' fast,
  Enthroned among his fellow men.

---

* Alexander Lumsden, a singularly robust, and, in one or more ways, a
somewhat remarkable man, the father of the writer, died, overcome with
agricultural disasters, and domestic calamities of an exceptional kind, on
the 9th March 1888, at East Linton ; and was buried as above at Prestonkirk on the 12th of March, a very large concourse of the whole people
following his remains to the grave.

The sceptre in his hand, it was
  The carle stalk—integritie ;
His croon was truth, an' for his cause
  He claim'd the friend of right to be.

With stern, but kind and valiant mien,
  Owre life's high way he march'd alang ;
Whate'er he wist, he gain'd, I ween,
  With resolution fix'd an' strang.

But sicker ills pursued the king,
  His lofty crest was stricken low
A thousand times, but nocht could bring
  That regal heart despair to know.

Thro' wreck an' ruin, woe an' want,
  Wi' steadfast nerve he held his way ;
Nor age, nor pain, nor death could daunt
  That matchless spirit to this day.

Wi' breaking hearts we leave him here,
  Oh, may his sleep be deep an' blest !
For never on earth's rounded sphere
  Did truer man or stronger rest.

EPISTLES.

TO A YOUNG WRITER.

[ON ROBERT BURNS.]

—:—

DEAR SANDY,—
   Of wark this nicht I'm clear an' free
To sey the promise gi'en to thee
   About the rhyme on Burns
That you an' Jock wish me to spin
'First time the Muse cries ' Sam begin !
   Your Fancy's hour returns!'"
Sae I hae ta'en my muckle chair,
   Ink, paper-scraps, an' pen ;
But what to scribble—I declare
   I trow na yet nor ken !
      Your scheme is, the theme is
         Sae loomin', lairge, an' hie,
      I nither an' swither,
         Till Peg maist tak's the gee !

For Burns is he wham every Scot
Gars bauld fire up an' glow red-hot,
   An' thrill frae tap to tae
For love an' pride o' auld Scot-land

His rugged Mither, wha doth stand
   Sae strang by freend an' fae.
Her thistles wagging owre the moor,
   Her daisies on the lea,
Her foaming streams, her mountains dour,
   Her rock-bound tumblin' sea,
      He sees a', an' gi'es a'
         A ready welcome dear,
      As soon as the name fa's
         O' Burns upo' his ear !

And up come visions efterhend
O' bluidy weir that Scotland kenn'd,
   Ere ever Bannockburn ;
And Wallace " red-wat shod !" he sees
Triumphant Scotia's standard heeze,
   And her usurpers spurn !
A ne'er-match'd wally wicht was he,
   Sae staunch he couldna steer,
As stark as Strength, as Freedom free—
   A Peer without a peer !
      A Pearl, a carle,
         Up-towering abune a' ;
      A Hero, whase marrow
         The haill wide warld ne'er saw !

He braucht the dawn, and Bannockburn,
The ae, lone star o' Freedom's morn,
   Did herald in the day,
Whan Liberty uprose as bricht
As a June sun that scatters nicht,
   An' scaurs the haurs awae !
Wi' flashing eye he sees the Bruce
   His marshal'd phalanx wave

Wi' war-brand in the closing truce
    To victory or the grave !
        Inspiring and firing,
        All hearts to do or die,
        And welcome, what will come—
        Red death or victorie !

As high for humble social Man
The Burns trumpet note was blawn
    His living pages through ;
Despite chance wealth or poverty,
He was (and would that a' should be)
    The natural man an' true :
A modest independent mind,
    A heart sincere an' free,
To live an' feel for a' mankind
    Wi' him aye bure the gree !
        And sure aye the poor aye
        In him a Wallace fand !
        Whase creed was, whase deed was
        By Worth alone to stand !

Wi' piercing, clear, prophetic eye
He saw the time fast drawing nigh,
    The coming Age of Right ;
The age of justice and content,
When wrong an' falsehood's power is spent,
    And love and truth have might !
The brotherhood and sisterhood .
    Inalienable of Man,
The victory of the wise and good,
    The universal plan,

Assign'd is, design'd is,
And fix'd by Heaven's decree,
Which timely, sublimely,
The " warld owre " yet shall see!

And seeing and believing this,
Frae first to last what was amiss,
And shored to block its course,
Wi' satire, of the power of fire,
He molten'd into laughter dire,
And stronger made the force
Of right and righteousness, that aye
Warm in his briest he nurst,
To throw, when time was ripe, and slay
All things to Man accurst—
Vain fashions an' passions,
Inhuman acts an' ills,—
Yea, a' wrang, that ere lang
Man's weal allures an' kills.

Sagacity, as her First Son,
And Heir o' a' her realms an' throne,
Hail'd Burns at his birth!
And, that he weel micht rule an' reign
For ages o'er her wide domain,
She ransack'd Heaven an' earth
For regal gifts to serve his needs,
And King-like him adorn,
Sae's a' his sov'reign words an' deeds
Nae man could scout or scorn ;
But surely, securely,
As treasures from above,
Believe them, receive them
In reason, faith, an' love!

F

Transcendent wit, an' sympathy,
Wide as the warld's sel', had he,
  And gifts divine of Sang ;
A soul of eloquence was his,
Where Harmony abode in bliss,
  And revell'd aft an' lang ;
Description's watch-tower was his eye,
  All Nature was her field,
Whase every limit, low an' high,
  Did to her pleasure yield ;
    Sae nappy, sae happy,
      Her limner drew—in sooth,
    His pictur's were victors,
      Whose "art" became as truth !

The myst'ries of the human heart,
The saul's dread chammers—to this "art"
  Disclosed their secrets a' ;
His ingine was a search-licht that
Their dark neuks made as clear, I wat,
  As noonday mak's the Law ; *
And this grim human heart an' saul,
  Whilk god-like he explored,
He turn'd at will into the Hall,
  And High Haunt of Concord.
    Thence, pinging, an' ringing,
      Its labyrinthines throo,
    His sangs rise to Paradise,
      Frae whilk at first they flew !

But conscience, Sandy !   Halt ! my lad !
Wot ye the time ?   The nicht has fled,
  An' Janwar's day creeps in,

---

* Traprain Law.

Just like a peevish auld gray man,
Wha ill this bitter cauld can stan'
    An' fain wad thow his shin !
Owre Airthur's Sait the growin' licht
    The rested toun revives ;
Laz'rus shogs aff the sloth o' nicht,
    Sair envying cosy Dives !
        And graphic the traffic
            Resumes its darg o' din,
        Sae, Sandy, aff hand, I
            Cry thee " Ta-ta !" an' rin.

TO A SHOEMAKER.

—:— -

ALL HAIL, thou king of leathern bales,
    Behold ! thy subject, " Sam," to-night
    Before thee falls—that is, to write
Anent thy note on human ails,
    And answer, as he best may dow,
    The sage thoughts of thy sapient pow.

Thy charge—" That all is ruled by chance
    Is proved by men's unequal lots "—
    Is just as wise as saying, " Coats,
And caps, and boots, brand-new from France,
    Are undesigned, and erring all,
    Because the big don't fit the small."

Does't shock thy tender soul to see
    " The good and true to ruin shied,
    While up life's sunny heights descried
The false and vile mount fast and free ?"
    Ah ! lad, this is but seeming ill,
    The fattest land's at foot o' hill.

" Some, whiles, by thunderbolts to earth
    Are struck ; by ruthless engines some
    Are crushed, or torn limb from limb ;
Many are maimed, or blind from birth,
    And countless creatures their life long
    Endure the pain of others' wrong.

" With purposed ill and accident,
    War, famine, massacre, disease,
    And ignorance—chief cause of these—
This world's way is darkly pent !"
    But even, with these full in thine eye,
    Can'st thou no god but chance descry ?

" Yon proud ship, mann'd with hopeful souls,
    To our white cliffs comes bounding home ;
    Just one night more to stem the foam
Ere into England's arms she rolls !
    Alas ! that one night more at sea
    Must mean for her—Eternity !"

Again, " the weirdly, dripping mine
    Beams and resounds with light and life,
    And workmen whistle at their strife,
Hopeful of rest and bright sunshine—
    When flash ! one flare of after-damp
    Puffs out for them Life's flickering lamp !"

Well, Dick, may not a " Father-God "
    Administer the seen, at least,
    By " fixed laws " which, observed, feast,
In this their nursery-like abode,
    His children all, to greatest gain,
    With disciplining peace and pain ?

I wot so.   " Accident " to me
    Is but a shell—the husk wherein
    A divine purpose is, to win
A rapid end : On land, on sea,
    The mightiest " fact," the meanest " dot,"
    Are both the guise of what's seen not.

Did e'en but one of all "God's laws"
   Provoke or effect ill—obeyed—
   Then might thy creed be not gainsaid,
And pessimism find good cause ;
   What then, if they but good afford
   All round—unbroken, unignored ?

I may not say that "evil" all
   Is the result of broken law ;
   Evil there is, and it may draw
And train to strength man's virtues small ;
   Your craft would little skill disclose
   But for our need of boots and shoes !

So then, O King, to close with thee,
   Be not so sure of what thy brain
   Suggests when sadly o'er Life's main
Hope flies thy sight, for nought can be
   More certain than that human wit
   Disclaims those marks it fails to hit.

TO A YOUNG COMMERCIAL FRIEND.

[THE NEW AND THE OLD WAYS TO " WEALTH."]

—:—

THOU writ'st me, Jack, o' thy intent
   To " win an independence,"
An' pray'st, wi' " advice," I anent
   Thy purpose dance attendance :
For Auld Langsyne, see " Samuel," then,
   As thy fond love beseeches,
Clank doun, an' point wi' ready pen
   The shortest cut to riches !

Begin wi' slichtin' ilka friend
   A cast aneth thy " station,"
Frae poortith's neives thy kids defend
   As ruinous degradation !
An' every " chum," though true an' staunch,
   Gin thou in gear o'ermatch him,
Straight from thy favour—root an' branch—
   Without a tear detach him.

To add ane boddle to the hoard—
   (That " privilege independent ! ")
Ne'er grudge to truckle to a lord
   As low as he's transcendent !
Obsequious, court the monied loons,
   Lip-worship and adore them—
Wi' subtile flatt'ry busk their crouns,
   An' flower the ground before them !

Peer out, wi' keen politic e'e,
    The *a la mode* incomin' :--
So shall thy Protean morals be
    Found meet when 'Change shall summon !
Like full-blawn ship, tak', then, the seas,
    Prank't in the blaze o' fashion ;
An' tack to ev'ry blast an' breeze
    Of " nobby " vice an' passion !

A free, accepted, favour'd son,
    A weel-graced bairn o' Mammon,
What thou despise thou needna shun,
    Nor what see'st fause ca' gammon.
Thine ain belief, lock't in thy heart,
    Do resolutely fate it,
Absolve thy soul the good man's part,
    Tho' heaven desiderate it !

To circumvent, or even draw
    To ruin the unwary
Be bold—ne'er fear thy country's law,
    Gif thousands are the quarry !
Dodge, plot an' shuffle, wind an' wheel,
    Work auld an' new pretences ;
Just thou succeed—outshame the de'il—
    Success a sure defence is !

*   *   *   *   *

Thus Moderns Mammon's hichts aft clim,
    Post on vile crime they sprawl up,
Auld wisdom's yoke 's owre lag o' limb
    Thae geniuses to haul up !

They maun mak' spangs at sudden wealth,
    Abjure as "loss" ways thrifty ;
Be millionaires by storm or stealth,
    Or fled bankrupts—at fifty !

An' gin the envied guerdon 's won—
    Alas, thou lord o' nature !—
"Self made" art thou !— Ah ! self-undone—
    One moment scan the creature :—
Lo ! prematurely auld an' spent,
    " A conscience but a canker ! "
In " independent " discontent,
    The Knave finds sorry " anchor ! "

Dear Jack, deep ponder this a wee—
    The " self-made " rogue's repletion ;—
Then, sure, thine after aim shall be
    A nobler far ambition !
For competence the brave will fight,
    Nor worlds in arms debar them ;
But, want or wealth, they follow right,
    Tho' yawning death would scaur them.

Adieu ! I shun that higher ground,
    Where best I might exhort thee ;
But holy themes let priests expound,
    " Sam's " rhymes they 'd ill comport wi'.
Go on an' prosper to the end,
    Auld honour put thy trust in !
Heed not what meed this world send,
    Heaven metes at last the just ane !

TO THOMAS PINTAIL, ESQ.

—:—

DEAR TAMMAS,—
  I got your note. Fell proud I be
To learn you're on our " Comytee,"
" We've got a judge and referee "—
  (Cried I, richt vauntie !)
" In our polemic dominie,
   W'uth ony twenty ! "

Now shall each daurin' candidate
Be heckled weel on Kirk and State !
John Calvin's creed—the " five points " great
  They maun endorse 'em !
Armenian heresies on " fate "
  Avoid—or curse 'em !

Tackle them, Tam ! an' be nae sparin'
On that teuch doctrine—Trinitarian !
If in yer grips ae cheep, like Arian,
  They dare to mew—
Expunge them wi' the Unitarian
  Socinian crew !

Syne pruve them wi' the Athanasian—
That " creed " wi' ne'er a twa-faced phrase in ;—
Gif ane demur, ye'll spier nae reason,
  But pack him aff—
Folk hae nae mind, when barns are bleezin',
  To riddle chaff !

Oor need is urgent—therefore wale
A shepherd famed owre hill an' dale
For zeal, an' wrath, an' lungs to quail
  This stiff-neck'd age,
Wi' graphic notes on Clootie's jail—
  Its destined cage !

And, also, Tam, *I rede ye weel*
Yer choice be on a *Union chiel*,
Wha will go in for pawkie skill
  An' compromise,
Cannily to " bird-lime," " trap "—or steal
  A' prey that flies !

Noo warrin' patronage is gane—
Worried the auld contention bane—
Why should we, like three jowlers, strain
  At ithers' neck ?
Oh ! sune oor trinal leash—rin ane,
  For Scotland's sake !

Ye mooted " Disestablishment,"
An' spier hoo I think thereanent !
Ye ken fu' weel I'm that way bent ;
  But, Dominie !
'Tis that towards UNION it wud tent
  The sisters three !

An' lastly, Tam, mak' sure yer choice
Fa's on a lad wi' catchin' voice,
An' genty mien—fit to rejoice
  Our lasses fickle ;
Or ye may raise yer lugs—a noise
  Wad gar them tickle !

They doubly can out-vote the "men,"
Sae, gin ye widna toil in vain,
Mind what I say—'bune a', wale ane—
          A woman wanter ;
An' there's my loof !—the Manse, aff haun',
          Is his instanter !

TO RAB O' THE HILL.

[IN REPLY TO A CHARMING POEM BY MR ALEXANDER DONALDSON

("RAB O' THE HILL") OF GIFFORD, ENTITLED

"TWA WEE WEANS."]

--:—

" THEY toddle up an' doon the stair "
    Your twa wee weans ;
And there they'll toddle evermair—
    The twa wee weans ;
The " dainty cherubs " ne'er again
Shall leave fond Memory's sweet domain,
But ever in our hearts remain
    Your " twa wee weans."

Fa' blessings doun on you an' them—
    The twa wee weans ;
They canna help but bless your hame,
    Sich twa wee weans ;
To be the dad o' sic a pair
. I'd swap a hantle rhyming ware,
Syne point, defiant, dool an' care—
    My twa wee weans !

Tho' I'm a stranger to you a',
    And your wee weans,
I wadna fear to swear ava
    The twa wee weans

Were bonnier than flowers in May,
Sang sweeter than a laverock's lay,
And innocent as lambs at play—
    Your twa wee weans.

I fancy noo, an' think I see
    Your twa wee weans
Trot but an' ben in merry glee—
    Twa rare wee weans ;
Their little cheeks—the budding rose,
Their saft blue eyes—the violet shows,
And snawy white the seraph brows
    O' your wee weans.

Their daddy sits and bids the wife
    See their wee weans,
And prizes higher than his life
    Sich sweet wee weans ;
For then he'll act the man, and be
A sturdy struggler, firm an' free—
Nae weakly fool shall faither ye—
    My twa wee weans.

Fareweel ! my couthie, canty chiel,
    An' your wee weans ;
I ken your heart beats true an' leal
    For thae wee weans ;
I havena felt for weeks afore
As when your rhyme I read it o'er—
They moved me to the vera core,
    Your twa wee weans.

TO THE MAN IN THE MOON.

--:—

ALL HAIL ! high ancient patriarch—
Antediluvian Man,
Wha needed nae auld Noah's Ark
When the dreidfu' Flude began ;
But viewed the waxing storm o' rain,
Nor cared ae pinch o' snuff ;
" Cah ! lat it rain, droon hill an' plain,"
Quoth thou, " *I'm* safe enough ! "

When elfins lea' the breaks an' shaws,
To trip their fairy round ;
With howlets in auld castle wa's,
Thou hold'st converse profound.
And whan, amang the stars sae bricht,
The braid moon tak's the field,
There, plain, thou look'st by warlock slicht,
The device on her shield.

And, sicht o' yearth 'tis aft to see
Thy grand career on high !—
A roving Scotch wind blawin' free,
A Scotch November sky !
The star o' morn blinks i' th' west,
Bricht in its patch o' blue,
Till, dim owreheid, thou slip'st to rest.
Whan our Rab yokes the ploo.

Ride on ! bauld Lunar artiste, ride,
    Thy car 's baith gilt and brent ;
This warld is thy grand circus wide,
    Thae heavens themsel' thy tent :
Mankind, thy audience fit below,
    Cheers on with fit guffaw ;
Thou art their monarch fit, I trow,
    They—thy fit subjects a' !

TO MY LANDLORD.

[THE AGRICULTURAL DEPRESSION.]

—·:—

PEACE, weal, an' wealth, an' length o' days,
  Wi' leal Scots love an' honour,
Combine an' bring a' happiness,
  Your lordship o' the manor !
Excuse this blaud, tho' poor always,
  And all obscure its donor,
His rustic Musie pleads an' prays,
  Ye'd ne'er for this disown her.

(Her screed's nae threat'ning missive sent
  By Parnell-fired Hibernian,
To shore ye death as punishment
  For drawing rents agrarian :
Scotch to the core !—nae compliment
  Gin *she* lilts " sense " unvaryin',
And relegates the violent
  To Fenian an' barbarian !

But noo, my lord, she'd fain ye'd ken
  She's dounricht sair distressit ;
Her wut—in degrees—aucht or ten
  'Neath zero I should guess it :

G

In truth, the drap ink in her pen
　　Seems frozen wi' distress o't,
An' sair she dreads my parl'd brain
　　This yarn will mak' a mess o't).

＊　　＊　　＊　　＊　　＊

Cumbrous restraint frae tacks out-weed,
　　An' root out auld hypothec ;
Entail, an' a' the land law breed
　　That plague us waur than toothache !
And compensation grant, indeed,
　　" Improvements " tho' not shoe thick,
An' gie to land, like grub, free trade,
　　So's a' may buy an' ploo quick !

And when a's dune, my lord, sure then
　　We'il laugh the Russ an' Yankee—
They may as weel as us cry " hain !"
　　The rocks o' Killiecrankie.
A fair field gie to Scottish men,
　　Your favour keep, an' thank ye ;
An' gif they downa stand their ain,
　　The di'el plays them a pranky.

But, oh ! my noble lord and chief,
　　What will or then betide us ?
This crisis like a midnight thief,
　　Is in the house a-side us.
That foreign rung in's neive is prief,
　　Destruction maun abide us,
If landlord mercy some relief
　　Does not aff-hand provide us.

In common times 'twad men degrade
    To hint or crave abatement ;
That all should 'bide their bargains made,
    Is truest doctrine statement.
But there are pits in every trade,
    And some that seem by fate meant,
To swallow whole the best rules laid
    For trade's true honest treatment.

An' this is ane, my lord, the noo—
    The pitfa' term'd " Depression ; "
An ugly, black quagmire to view,
    But uglier to play clash in !
Yet heid an' lugs, a droonin' crew,
    This bog the farmers plash in ;
Some hope the strong may struggle thro',
    But *sinkin'* here's the fashion.

Here, then, my lord, your bard's appeal !
    Exceptional our strait is ;
So, in the way ye ken sae weel,
    Exceptional grace do mete us !
A chieftain—let your people feel,
    Tho' high o'er their's your state is,
To meanest clansman's woe an' weal
    Your chieftain's heart elate is.

Remember in your castle ha',
    Whaur never poortith dare look,
When in your princely rents ye draw,
    What a' they cost your puir folk.
In simmer's sun an' winter's snaw,
    For duds an' brose a queer lock,
They toil'd in hundreds, grit an' sma'.
    To heap your burstin' gear-pock.

Abridgement o' a half-year's rent
    Would scarce suffice to ease us ;
And not e'en three times ten per cent,
    Discounted, would release us.
It seems to " Sam," then, what we want,
    An' in lang-run micht please us,
Is—to revalue by consent,
    An' tak' what justice gi'es us.

Choose each a fittin' arbiter,
    The Shirra he another,
An' let them fix a rent that's fair,
    Without mair bosh or bother.
This micht mak' a' our jealous stir
    In mutual goodwill smother,
An' laird an' tenant—hand an' fur—
    Like auld naigs pull together.

Farewoel, my lord ! this humble strain
    In its ain spirit tak' it,
Judge not its counsel wi' disdain
    Because a clod-poll spak' it ;
But, whether by you scorn'd or ta'en,
    Till some ane better mak' it,
The feck o' folk—this time again—
    May side wi' " Mucklebackit ! "

TO A PLOUGHMAN.

—:—

DEAR JAMIE,—
  Thy letter duly cam' to hand—
Thou'st clark'd like a scholar grand !
Quoth I, " He wields the writer's brand—
    Wi' fell wit spear'd !"
Syne leuch, to think my native land
    Such peasants rear'd.

Thy reasons for the plooman's way,
To seek new hames each term day,
Almost convinced me thine essay
    Was Wisdom's voice—
But, based on premises astray,
    It's just " mere noise."

For the big bulk o' ploomen chiels,
'Tis fated—they maun till our fiel's ;
This is their certain lot, which wills
    The Powers Eterne ;
And, health an' breid, wi' a' its ills,
    'Tis nae sae stern.

I grant at times it may be richt—
Even necessar' in mony a plicht—
Our dear auld hames and haunts to slicht
    For guid, for aye ;

But what about the general flicht
    Each term day ?   ·

In auld times " hinds " were valued at
Sae much a heid—nor much at that—
Like needfu' owsen, dowg, or cat,
    They war " retained,"
And, toiling like the brutes, I wat,
    They brute pay gained.

But this is changed, or changing fast,
The " slave's chain " clanks but in the past,
Man's coming to his " right " at last
    The warld owre,
And only tyrants backward cast
    · An envious glower.

But if true independence brings
Free will, free speech, and ither things—
As cash and dignity—it flings
    Nane's dues aside,
Nor with a sneer insolent stings
    A maister's " pride."

Nae " maister " either in his station
Should mak' o' this new dispensation
A vantage ground—all obligation
    Henceforth to slip,
And, with his bare " remuneration,"
    The workman clip.

But, Jamie, be thou leal an' chaste,
And tak' a true freen's word in haste,

Stick whaur ye be !   Blaw not like waste
    Life's common o'er !—
The wheat soon rests—the chaff amaist
    Flits evermore.

TO A FRIEND IN AMERICA.

[AFTER A WET YEAR.]

—:—

ꟽEAR M———,
  Hoo are ye a', man, owre the Ferry ?
O' thee I aft think an' Fort Garry,
And ferly gin Time's restless wherry
   Shall e'er again
Waft us thegither, bauld an' merry,
   Some glorious e'en !

Lang in the backwoods we twa ran,
Defying skaith, clime, beast, or man,
Adventure in our hearts, in haun'
   A Colburn rifle—
All friendless, in that strange long lan'
   Deeming a trifle.

Sin syne, auld comrade, I am here ;
But this by thee seems not to lear',
As in your dear-prized note ye speer—
   Gin "Peg" I'd mount—
O' this far-famous awfu' year
   Some true account.

I'm stagger'd whereat to begin,
The tale sae far, far back does rin,

But I'll just jump my story in
    Where last hairt ended,
And first the deluge, like a linn,
    On us descended.

A' winter, lowlands, haughs, an' glens,
Were transform'd lochs, an' bogs, an' fens ;
Even weel-drain'd upland, loamy plains
    In your auld kintra,
Up to midsummer, wi' the rains,
    Kythed deserts wintry.

Sma' wheat was saun, an' maist o' that
Was droun'd out to a waesome scrat
Ere Mayday cam', like ominous bat
    Wi' cloudy wings,
To usher in the nicht distraught
    This harvest brings.

A' thro' the spring, the Land o' Cakes
Ne'er buskit her auld shaws an' brakes ;
But storms an' multitudinous wrecks
    Clad her in woe ;
An' for birds' sangs, we'd bardies' shrieks
    'Bout " Dolereaux ! "

Trowth ! drear an' gurly was the simmer !—
Puir nature ! May month wadna trim her ;
June whistled thro' her leafless timmer
    Like surly March,
And e'en July, the turn-coat limmer,
    Proved hard an' harsh.

St Swithin's Day stole on apace,
Great promise in its watery face,
The legendary tale he'd grace—
    The " forty days,"
Like water kelpies, each in 's place,
    Beyond gainsays.

A month ahin', at lang an' last,
'Tween showers, an' gales, an' skies o'ercast,
And sick hope daily sinking fast,
    The hairst began,
When lo ! anither horror pass'd
    Owre auld Scotland.

A flood, to whilk the floods afore—
An', trust me, we had score on score !—
Were but as gutters to the roar
    An' rackin' din
O' spated Tyne's tumultuous pour
    Owre Linton Linn.

The Craps ?   I beg thee, dearest M———,
Constrain me not to talk o' them,
For if sae, ye'd my screed condemn
    As patent lees ;
And deem a madman grown auld " Sam "
    Athort the seas !

Sae warrily, I'll simply say,
We've gat our hairst a' in this day ;
And we've some forty stacks o' strae
    Forbye the chaff ;
As for the corn, baith guid an' gray,
    Is just some draff.

The tatties ? Wae's me for the tatties !
For, tho' not fond o' them as Pat is,
I railish them wi' herring as saut as
              Yerl Beconsfiel' ;
But, och, this year, alas ! their faut is
              Sae few to peel.

The nceps an' them are just a match,
Wi' here an' there a guidish patch,—
Of failure absolute a swatch
              The best I've seen
Sin daylicht, suffering, drew the latch
              O' "Sammy's " eyne.

Fareweel, dear Malcolm, fare ye weel !
God bless ye a' ! And thou, dear chiel,
Should e'er blind Fortune's chancy wheel
              Ligg us thegither,
Wow ! what a glorious nicht we'd steal
              Frae care an' bother !

SECOND EPISTLE TO A FRIEND IN AMERICA

—:—

BRAW thanks for thy fraternal letter,
   Pack'd, line on line, wi' priceless matter,
A' sorts o' news an' dear-prized clatter
     'Boot a' our freen's,
Wha mak' a Scotland owre the water,
     The auld demeans !

   *   *   *   *   *

" How are the times in Caledon—
I ask not of thy god, Gladstone !—
But how's the farming moving on ? "
     Thou eager question,
And sagely threep the theme is one
     " Sam " shouldna jest on !

Here, then, thou brand-new wondrous saunt,
Since gravity is now thy cant,
Know that this Scottish year is scant
     Of naught ;—it seems
A medium-yielding, average plant,
     Sans all extremes.

The spring cam' soughin' saftly in,
Our seed was sawn wi' dry March win';

May sapless sped; but left behin'
　　A faultless braird,
Whilk June and July matured syne
　　With meet regard.

Now hairst is ended ; thack an' rape
Secure a sonsy, weel-won crap
Against the rains, an' ocht mishap
　　Frae winter's storms—
God send it scare beyond high Alp
　　Last year's alarms !

The neeps an' tatties, too, are prime
No free o' blight—but just a styme ;
We scare a hopefu'er autumn time
　　Have known before ;
Had we 'scaped recent loss—this " rhyme "
　　I'd sung galore !

Alake, alake ! there hangs a tale
The stoutest, hopefu'est heart might quail !
Scores o' our sturdiest farmers fail
　　To jouk the jaw,
An' broken-hearted families haill
　　Gae to the wa' !

What heart but bleeds to think o' them—
Wives, bairnies, auld stumps—sire and dame—
A' riven oot their auld, auld hame
　　They've kenn'd sae lang,
To seek in tears, despair an' shame,
　　Some-whare to gang !

And active, pushing fallows, too,
Have bit the dust—alas, nae few !—
But cases such as theirs, I trew,
    Move pity less,
Because themsel's, wi' rack-rent, drew
    Themsel's a mess.

A' owre the land, this is the tale—
Failures an' changes thick prevail ;
Land-rent is melting down like hail
    In April's lap ;
An' mony farms the lairds themsel'
    Perforce maun crap.

But efter a' is said an' dune,
The gloom, I ween, will lichten sune,
The mirkiest hour—whan there's nae mune—
    Precedes the daw'—
.A jiffey ere god Sol abune
    O'erwhelms it a' !

Like water running unconfined,
A' things to level are inclined ;
Sae rents will settle—cash or kind—
    As need shall show,
Tho' twenty million lairds combined
    To stem the flow !

Then welcome thy steam argosies,
In smoking fleets out owre the seas !
Send meat an' wheat or what thou please,
    To staw toom bellies :
'Twill cost thee sune a Yankee " squeeze "
    To undersell us !

A fair field and no favour granted,
We'll face old Jonathan undaunted,
An' laugh his " boundless prairies," vaunted—
        " Heaven's maps unfurl'd ! "
John Bull's an' Sandy's pluck 's implanted
        To whip the World !

Adieu ! mine erewhile backwoods' crony,
I lang to meet ye mair than ony !
Oh, tak' a whid to Scotland bonnie
        Some canny morn—
Thy sicht wad heeze her higher than mony
        Braw craps o' corn !

Fareweel 'enoo ! whate'er betide
To us the " Ferry " either side,
Or weel or wae the warld wide
        By turns dow tak' it,   .
I am, auld comrade, friend, an' guide
        Thine—" Mucklebackit ! "

TO A RETIRED DOMINIE.

[ON " CREMATION."]

—:—

COME ! yet yaul Thomas len's yer lug,
Whyles I a friendly neb an' mug,
In its grim portals deftly plug,
    Sans botheration ;
An' a' this tale unravel rugg
    Anent " Cremation."

This age materialistic—whilk
Developed prime a Mill and Dilke ;—
Deems far waur than sour kirn milk
    Your auld warld lear' ;
Its mental kine o' *Savan* bulk
    Crave fierier fare.

So " free-thought " horn'd, these later bulls,
Wha rive auld Nature to the hools,
In pastures new, wi' " laws " an' " rules,"
    Outshame the moon—
Tracin' shrewdly fathership o' fools
    To a baboon.

Thus follows it, as wrack frae wind,
(Effect its cause comes slap behind),
These sages " meek," in pride of mind,
    Sing out—" Behold !
Burial, this day, doth Science find
    Is waste untold."

"Science," at length declares, alas !
Water, carbonic acid gas,
Ammonia, an' a little ase,
        We a' maun be !
As food for plants—kail-stocks or grass—
        After we dee !

And, strange to say, the way to do't
Is *burnin'* !—burnin' croon an' cloot—
No' as they did auld witches—but
        In pats or pans,
Frying us to cinders when red hot
        Like herrin' rans.

Then fareweel, Tam, our auld kirkyaird,
Its tear-bedewed an' bonnie swaird,
And a' its memories revered,
        Wrench frae our hearts ;
Syne of the rest we'se be na fear'd
        To play our parts.

Oh ! Tam, auld Tam ! gie me yer loof !
Age on your pow now snaws sad proof,
That what o' life for your behoof
        A dwindling shair'd
Is only left !—e'en just enough
        To say ye're " spared ! "

D'ye think, auld Tammas, when ye dee
(As dee ye *maun*—next week, may be),
That ye'd prefer your friends to see
        Ye buried decent ?
Or that the crabbit dominie
        Should bleeze a crescent ?

If that the latter, mak' ye sure
That at yer burnin' will be there
Fu' mony a lad ye skelpit sair —
  To show " respeck,"
Smilin', as lowes ascend in air,
  To hear ye crack !

But mirth aside, I doubt this dream
Is jimp fit matter for my whim ;
Tho' serious hardly I can deem
  The ghaistly question—-
An' muckle jalouse 'tis a theme
  To crack a jest on.

TO THE REV. DR WHITELAW.*

[A REPLY TO "A PLEA FOR CREMATION."]

—:—

WELL hast thou shown, my gifted friend,
    Thy meet desire by fire to end !
For that thou should'st anticipate
The general doom—man's future fate—
Is just what I would have expected,
Who long thy genius have respected !

Yet still, my gifted friend and seer,
I pray the Fates thy wish sincere,
To be burn'd up—alive or dead—
May not be granted with fell speed !
But that thou may'st for many a year yet
Escape " fire-cars "—baith bouk and spirit !
To bless and gratify us long
With many a sermon, book, and song,
Ere to the chauldron thou art turn'd—
Into some white ash to be burned !

Thy reason—that as from fire proceed
All things whatever—quick or dead—
Seems rather far-fetched—that therefore,
We straight should bar the kirkyard door

---

* The late Rev. Dr Whitelaw, of Athelstaneford, East Lothian, who
wrote the " Plea " in the " Dublin University Magazine."

Against the sexton, and the pack
Of dingy " undertakers " black,

By emulating Mary's fame—
Consigning young and old to flame !
Kindling the monstrous human pyre
Behind some alley, barn, or byre,
And thrusting thither in a box—
Fired to a white heat till it smokes—
A brother, sister, parent, friend !—
Like divine Shelley —at whose end,
On that fair shore of Spezia's Bay,
Byron saw in blue flame melt away
Frame of the most ethereal mind
That ever linked with human kind,
And sicken'd in his soul to see,
The dread, infernal tragedy !

Again, wherever most abounds
Thy fav'rite element—in the rounds
And zones and climes of tropic heat—
There thou discover'st all that 's great
In the wide field of man's estate ;
There bigots, blackguards, despots, rage
Like starving lions 'scaped their cage ;
There are the rack, the wheel, the hook,
And other toys we overlook ;
There frowns the lover in fine style
When faithless maiden stirs his bile,
And ere he tramps her to the death,
In the heroic way thou saith ;
There, too, upon her funeral pile
Jumps up the widow with a smile !

" Disdaining, in extreme of joy,
Even to mourn her orphan'd boy ! "

Well, well !—The Lord I gladly praise,
If in the north such deeds as these
We vainly search for ;—but, I fear,
Even in this icy hemisphere,
Whether of Saxon, Dane, or Gael,
Our annals tell as bad a tale ;
Nay, even in times contemporaneous,
We see our records miscellaneous,
Teem daily with a mass of crime,
As hellish as of any clime
Beloved by Sol—the god of fire—
As any Christian should desire !

Mayhap we cannot boast those " rare
Stern virtues," which, in lands more fair,
Do " bloom as in a heavenly air."
What then ? sure that 's no reason why
Our friends should burn us when we die !
If 'tis our climate's fault, it seems
Bad taste, that we, by those same beams
We sadly lack'd in life, should be
At death despatched so terribly !

But seriously. Down from thy " Manse "
Look not, my brother, so askance ;
Love thou the tombs more tenderly,
And view them with untroubled eye !
They are the spots, of all the earth,
Most sacred. Altar, home or hearth,
Or battlefield—where Liberty,
Thro' war's riv'n clouds, hail'd Scotland free,

Have not such influence to enthrall
Or draw thought to them, as withal
Those green and silent mounds possess
Down through all life's mysteriousness !

Then, cherish still our " Auld Kirkyard,"
Its tear-bedewed and love-pressed sward ;
Its hallow'd memories revere
With reverent soul and heart sincere !
Care nothing for its rayless gloom—
Thy soul shall never know the tomb !
Turn not from it in coward fear,
But trust it more as death draws near !
Invoke no visions of crossbones,
Death's heads, or worms beneath its stones ;
But look upon " God's Acre " as
The porch through which to Him we pass !
The bed where we lie down a-weary
Of tumult vain and sorrow dreary,
To wake above, renew'd for aye,
The heirs of everlasting day !

TO DR R. BROWN OF BIRKENHEAD.

[THE AUTHOR OF AN APPEAL AGAINST DISESTABLISHMENT, AND
AN OLD SCHOOLFELLOW OF THE WRITER'S.]

—:—

TWICE o'er, old fellow, through and through,
 Your bookie I've perused in view
O' the "just notice, or review"
  I'm ask'd to send—
A kind critique, yet strictly true,
  As friend to friend.

The Auld Kirk's cause, in chapters ten,
You argue wi' a subtle pen,
" Establishment," ye apprehen',
  " Is her true weal,"
And surmise when she tints *that*—then
  She's wed the Deil !

Ye'd deem the pow that plann'd that blow
That o' the Auld Kirk's greatest foe,
Unwitting all if she'd forego
  Loof o' the State,
She soon her auld sel' scarce might know—
  Sae grown and great !

That's so ! And it just comes to this :
If Scotland thinks her Kirk amiss,
Then, though ye scribes in crowds cry " hiss !"
  The Kirk shall fa'—
That is *establishment*—and kiss
  Her new-made law !

Indeed, 'tis granted by yoursel'—
Page twenty-fourth, ye'll mind it well—
Your vera words ring like a bell
    Here pat an' prime,
An' toll your hollow logic's knell,
    Ev'n in my rhyme !

You say that—" We—the people—made
The Kirk State-bound, all unafraid
Of priests or princes in the trade
    Of freedom's foes ;"
By what right, then, are we gainsaid
    Thae bands to lowse ?

You dub us " persecutors," for
By righteous means we'd fain restore
To the whole nation as before
    The nation's funds !
Sure, Doctor, now thy wit in store
    Rins near the grunds !

Your ither reasonings I like better,
And some endorse as soundest matter,
Tho' even in them ye less than flatter
    Chiefs o' our Party,
And even D. M. L. bespatter
    Till he looks clarty !

To me the subject o' " statistics "
Is ane o' those I term " the mystics,"
But sums in your book hit like fist-sticks
    In Paddy's neive,
When freend or fae come in for their licks,
    Sans let or leave.

But you're for Union. *There*, my freen',
I shake hands wi' you, fast an' keen !
And ferlie if we strive to gain
  The same grand goal ?
Tho' *how* to reach it still has been
  As hard 's the Pole !

Could Union be "discovered" now,
Sans Disestablishment, I trow,
I'm not the Iconoclast 'twad throw
  The Kirk her eyric,
But rather her spread wings below
  I'd nestle cheery !

" But this can never be "—so I,
Being all for Union, fain would try
(What's coming certain by-and-bye,
  Despite "Appeals ! ")—
The grand "unstateing" remedie,
  Whilk "cures—or kills ! "

Fareweel, auld playmate ! Braw, braw thanks
For your grand book ! Whilst I'm on shanks
I'se ne'er forget ye—nor the pranks
  We play'd lang syne !—
Twa funnier fouters frae its banks
  Ne'er fish'd the Tyne !

MISCELLANEOUS POEMS AND VERSES.

THE FOPPISH YOUNG FARMER.

—:—

VIEW him at market with mustachioed face,
  Assuming manners which he cannot grace !
Affected, magisterial, insolent—
His landlord's fawning flunkey for a rent !
(That is prospectively—the pup I draw
Owes all his lustre yet to " poor papa.")
With lesser farm, his neighbour near is *dirt*
He'd scorn to recognise ; but, all alert
To puff his vanity, he'll stretch as high
E'en as my young lord in his London fly.
For one mere distant bow from one so great,
Our embryo husbandman would strangle Fate,
Tramp through the wheat to catch him at the turn,
Or for his " good day " ford waist deep Tyne Burn !
  See him at market : From this window here
The Rhymer spots him in his gorgeous gear !
The peacock's in full tail—behold the Flam—
The Duke of Puppeydom, the Prince of Sham !
And such an officer ! Ye'd think ye saw
The living Bismarck giving Frenchmen law !

While, all the time, in solid worth and power,
Yon mason's 'prentice, whose trade craft's his dower,
Towers o'er him as the giant forest oak
Does o'er the nettle or the wanton dock !
With swaggering strut see him parade the streets,
All smirks and bows for each " great man " he meets.
A local lord he salutes with an arm
Like bending boat-mast swaying in a storm ;
The Burgh Sires and Councillors, grown fat
On sweet authority, or Bernard's maut,
Are all his rage, his hob-nob friends, 'twould seem—
Ah, bless you, reader ! this too's just a whim
Of vanity ! Our knight they only know
By name or *custom*, which is here below
The " Open, Sesame !" to the closed world's heart,
And short-lived honours of the street and mart.
The " ladies," too, our Spark does deftly greet.
Veneered with pride, but few points of him meet
Their passing gaze ; besides, angelic eyes
See good in all things either side the skies.
Yet, doubtless, there is one whose *discreet* mind
Deems him a *catch—all* " true love " 's not sand blind.
His form is stalwart, if his mind be mean,
And his farm home— why, it might serve a queen ;
Beaux, too, like nags, are scarce, and one's oft glad
Not to be nice, but bit what can be had !
    A little while, our Hero starts for home,
The Rhymer follows.—Up in May's blue dome,
Sol, all secure, a long arc yet can sight
Ere Dian shall awake and supersede him quite.
    The farm is reached, the stylish drive is o'er ;
We join " young master " at the big-house door,
Then saunter with him through his brairded fields,

Quiet smiling at the pleasure which it yields
This rural princeling thrum the gamut o'er
Of self-laudation, and the treasured store
Of puerile nonsense, anent mean details,
And petty incidents—the shreds and tails
Of simple farming—telling all the trash
Like one divulging plots that might a nation smash !
 To test him in his own line, we enquire—
" Why weeds thrive most when cultured plants expire ?"
The response is—a vacant stare ! 'Tis vain
One crinch of wisdom to attempt to gain
From one who knows this as his highest lore—
" ' Spur ' won the last race, ' Whip ' the year's before ! "
 All knowledge of this wonder teeming round—
The gather'd spoils of scientists profound,
The splendours of the god-like Shakespeare—down
To the harsh ditties of the poet clown,
The annalist's strange tale, the problems sage
And vast—philosophic—with which our age
Is riven ; nay, the monthly storm and surge
Of wrath and balderdash within " *The George* "—
All to our Dandy are as unto one
Who lived before the flood—when schools and tawse
  were none !
 Now, should, my culprit, this too truthful *sketch*
Of thee meet thine own eyes, do further stretch
Thy patience—love whets the true censor's dart
That wisdom shoots. One word more, ere we part :—
 Because thou art thy father's son, and set
A *master* over men, deem thee not yet
The master of their thoughts—which measure thee
Intuitively just—where, if thou be
In them awanting, all thy lofty airs

Can never raise thee ! Arrogance impairs
What it would mend. Ah, grasp the better *rôle*—
Be *true*, if nothing great, for ev'n *thy* soul
Is worthy of this choice, tho' dwarfed and tame—
Son of thy father, father not his shame !
Nor deck thy cheek with *skin* humility,
But let thy very core and centre be ,
True modesty's own home ! Then whosoe'er,
World honour flaunts, doing thy falling share
Of honest work, the hairst will come anon,
When thou wilt reap in sheaves what thou in grains
    hast sown !

THE ADVENTURES OF BENJAMIN SOLOMON, YEOMAN, IN SEARCH OF A SPOUSE.

—:—

IN a light grey suit of West of England tweed,
    Bedight and garnish'd with kid mits and flower,
Behold our Solomon, rigg'd out on his steed,
    Ambling at twilight to his lady's bower.
Behold our " Ben," our annalist of threescore,
    The lover of three " dears "—two of whom " deid,"
He'd replace, like King Hal, with just one more,
    To cheer his gouty eld with love's sweet meed,
And warm his wintry nights, now wintry cold indeed.

Miss Park of Spott was in his eye—tho' she,
    Eighteen and pretty, had ne'er with him spoke—
If even, in fact, she knew such knight did be
    I would not swear by ev'n our Jubilee clock.
    But what was that to Solomon, douce folk ?
" Step out, old Floe ! what, weak wench daunton me ! "
    With that, and riding wild, the girth he broke,
And instant from his throne on Floe did flee,
Into a stagnant ditch—a noisome brock to see.

Old Floe, not in her prime—barring in wit—
    Grazed by the hedge (as oft she'd done before),
Until her master, Benjie, bit by bit,
    His slimy plight did full at length explore,
    Then long he rubb'd and scrubb'd, himself to fit

For love again; for, being so far, once more
Old Floe he'd mount, and, thereon doing it,
Set out again, like Crusader of yore—
By Sar'cen knock'd on head, much lower for his lore.

Gently he trotted, musing deep a tale
He'd tell Miss Kate; "How that his steed, being young,
Had bolted, bit in teeth, leaped fence and rail,
 Torn through forests, over crags had sprung,
 Like poor Mazeppa's, as by Byron sung,
Till on a *tattie bing* she last did fail
To make one inch more—when he quickly flung
Him from the saddle, as't had been the "Whale," *
And run for his dear life, to tell his love the tale!

Miss Kate was in the Old Lane—doing what?
 What other Kates have done since beaux would woo,
When Solomon burst up, broke the lovers' chat,
 And love's sweet spell that held the lovers true;
Told him gross lies with hand on heart, and blew
More monstrous sighs than ever fiend begat;
 Kate laugh'd, like waterfalls when May is new,
And thinking "such a lark," puffed Ben so that
She led him to the house like gander gone distraught!

His sad lorn love tale there he told, and, oh!
 Ere one brief hour, his troth was given and ta'en;
Then leaving him, to fetch before he'd go
 A "nip" and biscuit for her weary swain,
The merry Kate revolving in her brain
A merry trick to farce her feigned vow,
 Tripped to her lover, waiting in the lane,
And told him, as her laughter would allow,
The errand of old Ben, and all his lies and show.

---

* The famous monster one which was stranded and captured at Longniddry.

Then quickly in the chamber reappeared
    The maiden with decanter, cake, and all,
And pouring out a bumper round she veer'd,   ·
    And said, " Sweet : for my love drink this you shall,
    With one quick gulp place it beyond recall !
No excuse, darling, can this night be heard ! "
    Ben, in the third heaven, and fearing not a fall,
Pluck'd up the glass as 'twere a queen's reward,
    Stood on his feet, bow'd, drained the tonic gall—
For it was vinegar—but if he cared
The tears that streamed his cheeks told rather how he fared.

Then on the doorstep, too, his ardent flame
    Gat further quench'd, for, bidding him good-night,
Kate slapp'd his face, that fierier grew for shame,
    Then slamm'd and lock'd the door upon him tight.
    He could not choose, but mount old Floe, poor knight,
As down the avenue her steps proclaim ;
    But that night's cup he had not drunk yet quite,
For from among the bushes there now came
Kate's beau and others mask'd, to wreak on him their game.

They dragg'd him from the saddle—dress'd him out
    Like fish-wife from Dunbar, or Fisherrow ;
Remounted him, hand-bound, and legs about
And underneath they warp'd to ancient Floe,
Then cheer'd him for to find his home or no !

      *   *   *   *   *

Next morn at dawn, in Black's field, where both " nowte "
    And sheep did graze, ah ! such a woeful " show ; "
Solomon " in all his glory," 'midst the brute rout,
Bound high on Floe, a fish-wife, bearded, fresh from love's
    redoubt !

AT THE GRAVE OF A YOUNG FRIEND WHO WAS ACCIDENTALLY KILLED.

--:--

HE'S dead, this is his gravē !   Is then
      This a' we ken ?   Oh, I would ken,
In very fact, if thus my frien'
      Shall pass away ?
And here life's wondrous process en'—
      In kirkyard clay ?

In painful fancy, all intent,
From birth and upwards, stent by stent,
I trace thy strange "development,"
      To manhood's guise ;
When—world of wonder—death is sent,
      And here thou lies !

Are then thy twenty years in vain,
And a' thy parents' care and pain ?
Thy hard won lear ?—all life inane,
      Or as a feast,
At close o' whilk, death yawns "Amen,"
      An' sleep's the rest ?

Conjointly with thy brain's alway,
I traced thy "soul's" growth day by day ;
Now, here thy brain, compact of clay,
      Death-struck, dissolves.
But where that "soul" itself ?—away,
      'Yond our resolves ?

I

Is aught in Nature a vain boast?
Is aught in Nature ever lost?
Have not all things a purpose—most
         Even seen by man?
Where, then, is thine? not here, death crossed,
         Ere life's mid span?

In a' the works an' ways of God,
Discern'd alang life's devious road,
I thought—poor worm—injustice showed
         In much I saw;
Deceived by lack of power to prod
         His simplest law.

In a' we really understand—
Grains dropp'd from Nature's careless hand—
What wisdom, measureless an' grand,
         Astounds our view;
Proclaiming love's supreme command,
         A' Nature through.

Then, can this tomb the finale be,
O' a pure being such as thee?
If so—in thy sad death I see
         The rule despotic,
Of " chance," " mishap," or " destiny "—
         Blind, mad, chaotic.

It may be—but what tho' if 'tis?—
The fact that, whether woe or bliss,
The Ego finds in warlds than this
         (As here, indeed,)
For her a form corporeal is
         The first grand need.

What then, ye dull, material core ?
May not the Power, that from a spore,
Developed man, develop more—
        Than ye discern ?
Can ye wi' thy peep-glass explore
        The all eterne ?

Nae mair !   Here on thy grave, dear lad,
I'll wail thy fate, sae seeming sad,
While deeper thought gives deeper haud,
        Of faith by me,
And to my heart assurance glad
        'Tis well with thee !

Wail on, thou drear December win' !
Fa' doun, mirk nicht, an' close within
Thy blackest pall this warld o' sin—
        Death-beds and graves !
What reck we, gin we ken there's Ane
        Wha sees an' saves ?

AT THE AULD ABBEY BRIG.

[BELOW HADDINGTON.]

—:—

SAE as thou wert langsyne,
    Braid-sheeted, gleamin' Tyne,
Thou sweeps this hallow'd scene o' my life's early morn—
    Aye still the same fair stream,
    Tho' sair, sair's changed life's dream,
An' I'm a stranger grown i' the place whare I was born !

    As owre the brig I gaze,
    I'm lost as in a maze,
While the gloamin' breeze comes soughin' like the sound of
    the dead past ;
    And in the river clear,
    Dim, dusky shades appear—
The forms o' friends departed, by memorie fond recast !

    The weel-kenned banks I scan,
    The woods on either han' ;
The glimmering " Cascade," like a fair vestal's sheen ;
    The auld mill an' the weir,
    The kirkyard lone an' drear—
The white-wa'd ancient clachan, whare sae happy I hae
    been !

    Aneath me is the " Green,"
    And the dark, deep pool wherein
I hook'd my maiden trout ae memorable Fast-day ;

Wi' nervous joy an' fear,
Owre head I whisk'd him clear—
High through the middle air, some twa score yards away !

And there, by " Corbie Wall,"
Grew the spire-like spruce tree tall,
From whase cloud-stabbing tap I shook the May morn dew,
Reiving a starling's brood,
When, in owre careless mood,
I slipt my daring perch, an' swith cam' doun, I trew !

But ilka bush an' tree,
Bank, brae, an' grassy lea,
To " Sam's " fond sorrowing heart reca's its tale o' yore ;
To him a' Nature here—
Yearth, lift, an' atmosphere—
Are laden sick wi' memories o' the " days that are no
more ! "

Whaur's a' the auld folk flown,
That, thirty towmonds gone,
Ca'd this auld village " Hame," ere its last glory fled ?
Saved wi' the wreck, not ane,*
Alas ! is left behin',
Upo' the final exodus ae mournful gleam to shed !

Its Worthies, weel I min' !
Shae-cobblin', " Auld Corrine ! "
A veteran Peninsular, wha focht wi' Sir John Moore—
How keen was he to tell
O' the nicht his hero fell
When on pension days he quaffed a dram, and loud for
" grief " wad roar !

---

* A literal fact.

" Dick Scott ! " wee "Sandie Baird ! "
" Auld Steele ! "—anither caird
Frae that red pack o' Mars that o'er-ran Waterloo.
But, wow ; nae sot was he—
Owre stern an' proud to " spree,"
He strode a " soldier " to the last, majestical an' true.

Noo, ane an' a' are gane,
Fled, scatter'd, dead—alane
Here on the Brig I stand, an' muse on life an' death ;
The murmuring stream below
Wails like the voice of woe,
As I turn and face the wide warld, an' its lowering sturt
an' scaith !

THE FLITTIN' DAY.

—:—

AE sweet May morn, when blabs o' dew
    At bud an' blade were hingin',
An' larks, to hail the dawn anew,
    Spiel'd up the lift a-singing ;
'Twas then that I, my Peg to try,
    Slipt doun the auld green loaming,
To ane dear nook, beside the brook,
    Whaur sune I fell a-moaning.

A rumblin' like a yirthquake shook
    My simmer morning bourie ;
Sae I ran out, an' lap the brook,
    To see what was the stourie :
Alack, alack ! I stagger'd back,
    My bardie wrath forgettin'—
To learn its cause was cairts in raws,
    Wi' scores of puir folks' " flittin' ! "

On every road the heapit teams
    Swung hameward—rockin', noddin',;
The household gods portentous gleams
    Of instant wreck forbodin' !
But ropes an' strae conjoint that day
    Did haud in coalition,
Clocks, cradles, stools, beds, tikes, and dails,
    Secure—despite position.

A-tap the cairtloads, wives and weans,
　Crouch'd eerie an' dumfoun'ert;
I wat, weel shcuken were their banes,
　An' sair was mony a lone heart.
The grave gudeman, the "coo" in hand,
　Cam' soberly an' hinmaist;
But aft, I trew, nae crummie noo,
　As in past time was seen maist!

But what by ord'nar' look'd to ane
　That siccan scenes has view'd aft,
Was,—the new modes in plenishin',—
　Clocks, knick-knacks, grates, an' woodcraft;
Red polish gleam'd, veneerin' seem'd
　Nae real mahogany that day;
But easy chairs, and sofa lairs,
　Tauld plainly how the cat lay!

The lads haill clad, the lasses braw,
　An' deil o' either sickly;
My saul waxed proud to see them a'
　O' little drunts ne'er stickly.
A sturdier class will seldom pass
　Your traveller's view the same day—
Pith, body, sense, intelligence,
　And pluck ne'er lag nor lamely!

And seeing this, 'twere hard to tell,
　Why should be a' this "flittin';"
Sae straucht I speir'd the hinds themsel';
　Quoth they, as they'd been bitten :—
"Ye silly gowk! we farm folk
　(Could ye but comprehend it),
Some fyke's aye wrang—we're bound to gang—
　And hence we shift to mend it."

I answer'd, sadly, to mysel',
　Ye are the silliest gawkies,
To rive auld hames, 'mang frem to mell,
　For sic wheen triflin' mawkies !
D'ye think, quo' I, that heaven ye'll try
　When ance ye win the "new place?"
My lads, before, there's ill in store,
　And all unknown 's its true face.

Out o' the pan, intil the fire,
　Is neither fine nor fittin' ;
But even waur, despite desire,
　May be the wage o' "flittin'!"
What then, what then? again, again,
　Ye flit an' flit like Show-Jack ;
Till, some slee day, Death ca's to say—
　"Your final ' flittin' ' now mak'!"

An' musing thus, I daunder'd hame,
　Richt proud I wasna "flittin' ; "
Haith ! "Sam's " run plenty in his time
　To prize a cosh dounsittin' !
Auld Clover Riggs ! thy cleuchs an' craigs,
　Green haughs an' winding river,
As fixèd as thy castle wa's
　Be "Sam " to thee for ever !

WRITTEN IN THE COUNTRY.

[ON ANOTHER FLITTING DAY MORNING.]

—:—

THE flittin' teams I mark afar,
    An' froon upon this world's way ;
Our country neuk has been the star
    An' gem o' Scotia mony a day ;
Wha say her children are na free—
Ye gowks, ye gowks, come here an' see !

But are they wise wha freedom sae
    Accept in this nomadic style ?
Are they auld Scotland's staunch mainstay,
    Wha canna stay themsel's the while ;
But flit and flutter here and there,
Like bumbees that on nettles fare ?

I wat the wale o' our Scotch folk
    Hauds little share in this day's show ;
The feck o't is but scum an' brock,
    An' dregs up-jumlet from below ;
Whilk being licht, as froth is licht,
Maun e'en wi' the first puff tak' flicht !

For a' that, wha can weel deny
    What noble fellows, bane an' brain,
Some flitters are ! I gaze, an' sigh—
    "There's mair sides to this tale than ane."
That's sae ! an' just because it's sae,
We acquiesce, an' let it gae.

"WAE, WAE IS ME!"

—:—

IN my lone little cot in the suburb o' the toun,
 Musing to the music o' the wind's eerie soun'—
Brooding in a strange land on a' me an' mine,
How a' my joys hae fled wi' the days o' Langsyne.

To think I ance was Queen o' my ain faither's hame,
A bricht lauchin' lassie nae care wad tame ;
When Willie, dear, he woo'd me, an' won me for to part
Wi' the dear auld place an' that auld faither's heart.

O, shame befa' the fause friends that wiled Willie on
Frae his fireside and his Mary to their haunts about the
 toun ;
Sae happy for a year were Willie, dear, an' me—
O, that awfu', awfu' drink, that such a thing can be.

For a' things prospered then, an' oor little tot was born,
An' Willie was sae proud that birthday morn ;
Noo they baith sleep side by side—so dear, so dear to me—
In that strange kirkyard in this strange countrie.

A gloom fell owre the hame when Willie jee'd awa,
No' mony nichts a week—at first but ane or twa ;
But aye it deepened deeper that Storm he wadna see,
For the world was a' against him, an' he was changed to me.

O' waefu' was the douncome, waefu' was the fa' ;
Credit lost—a bankrupt—sald out house an' ha'—
Despair—disease—the mad-house, and onward wi' the wave,
Till the shatter'd wreck was sunken in a lowly pauper's
    grave.

O, my heart is like to break, my Willie, dear, to me,
An' wee Jamie, too, what gar'd my laddie dee ;
What gar'd my darling dee, when I only had but ane ?
O, Willie, Willie, Willie, we've pay'd the wage o' sin !

Noo to think that a' around me is blooming in the May,—
The green fields getting greener wi' the lengthenin' o' the
    day ;
The very birds so happy wi' their loves in ilka tree,
While lonely I maun wail—O, wae, wae is me !

The sun is in the far west enthroned on glowing gold,
My heart is wi' my dear ones in the kirkyard cold ;
When morning breaks so brightly o'er wood an' flowery lea,
It will break upon me wailing—wae, wae is me !

AULD CHARLIE.

[A FAVOURITE HORSE.]

—:—

AULD Charlie's deid, his yokin's out—
   I've kenn'd him sin' he was a cowte—
A nobler nag, a faithfu'er servan'
Yearth' ne'er bure, nor mair deservin'.
His lineage was obscure, I own—
A sort o' cross bred octoroon—
Frae nearest blood-royal pedigree
Removed even to the aucht degree ;
But in himself were gather'd neat
The virtues o' a' breeds complete !
And, sure, 'bune either looks or birth,
Even in horse flesh, ranks Moral Worth ?
An' this was Charlie's greatest " point "—
Guid nature, mense, an' " wut " conjoint !
In him dwelt neither wrath nor guile,
But leal desire to serve an' toil.
He wadna cruik'd a limb to harm,
Nor, kennin', trampit on a worm !
A cannier beast does no' survive him—
He loot our wee'st callant drive him.
Oh, proud as gipsy king on's cuddy,
How aft he rode him to the smiddy,
An' felt, when cock't upo' his mane,
As safe as mamma's cradled wean !
An' then ye could'na fit him wrang

In whatna yoke ye bade him gang—
Following or leadin', hand or fur,
Just what ye wish'd—he'd ne'er demur,
But, bricht an' ready, lithe an' free,
Gin ye were pleased, content was he.

Tho' but a "draught horse" was his end,
Yet his great service did transcend
His fate ; sae aftimes of a Sunday
A spankin' gig-hack, groom'd an' dandy,
Thro' foul and fair, mid-day or mirk,
Did he rin to and frae the kirk,
Hurlin' his maisters wi' a birr
That gart the sooplest " roadster " stir.

But now thou'rt deid, my peerless nag !
Sma' need is thine o' praise or brag !
Thy noble life I'se ne'er forget,
But in fond heart thy memory set.
And it is much, tho' deid in truth,
To have inspired this love an' ruth,
An' deep regard an' grief for thee,
Even in this sad extremity.

Only a horse—" a brute " thou wast,
But did stern justice mete at last
Deserving dues to nags an' men,
How were the tables turn'd then !
Some hantle o' our human kin',
I wot, would have to change wi' thine ;
An' the true " brute " would then be seen
Too often in Man's shape, I ween.

"AULD LEES."

[A RUSTIC PHILOSOPHER.]

—:—

SOME years ago, in the heart of East Lothian, I encountered, and afterwards became familiarly intimate with, a somewhat extraordinary character in the semblance, flesh, and actual being of a poor and hard-working farm servant, distinguished in those parts by the homely sobriquet of " Auld Lees "—his rightful designation being Jamie or James Lees. In any position of life this unique man would doubtless have been notable, but to my mind—considering his social status, his scant chances, and what he had intellectually mastered and made his own, despite his lowly origin and destiny—he was more remarkable than if, with better opportunities, he had risen, like others, to European eminence as an inventor or scientist.

A few years previous to my first knowledge of him, he had the shocking misfortune to lose his right arm by a threshing mill. His old master—no doubt knowing and appreciating his worth—retained him after the accident in his service, and at the time I became acquainted with him he filled the position of grieve, or steward, on a large arable farm. On this holding he likewise, for an extra perquisite, acted as general mechanic ; and despite the loss of his arm, he erected fences and kept in good repair all the gates and carts, threshing mill and engine, and the whole machinery on the farm. The cart mending, &c., he overtook during wet weather, and at other odd times when not engaged in the field ; and I have often stood by and watched him with intense interest while thus employed. On all those occasions he was invariably accompanied and assisted by a little schoolboy—a favourite son, or nephew of his own, I forget which ; and it was truly surprising to observe the workmanship executed, the invaluable and substantial result of the extraordinary methods and combined efforts of this original pair.

But, astonishing as these outside or professional operations of this man were, his mechanical, scientific, and other successes at home were even more so. He had been all his life not a mere reader only, but a voracious devourer, of books, magazines, and newspapers of all kinds—novels, politics, travels, histories, scientific works, &c.—in short, of all and of everything that he could possibly by hook or by crook buy, borrow, or in any way lay his eager hand upon.

He was a keen polemic and political partisan, a fluent, ornate, and pointed speaker—if not a born orator—and could harangue you by the hour in his native and expressive vernacular on any or all of the burning topics or favourite heroes of the day. He had made himself acquainted with far more than the simple elements of astronomy, botany, and biology, and was also deeply read in the geological lore of his time. His house was a singular combination of a hind's cottage, a chemist's laboratory, a circulating library, a millwright's workshop, and a scientific museum—a miscellaneous collection and repository of plant, animal, and rock " specimens ;" tools, retorts, books, maps, instruments, and other knick-knacks, too numerous to mention.

His grand study and hobby, however, when I first got acquainted with him, were the (to him) attractive problems of meteorology, or the "wauther science," in his own parlance ; and in pursuit of these he had actually constructed with his own hand all the appliances and instruments named in the annexed rhyme. This rhyme I wrote at his own earnest request, but for reasons which I need not here allude to, it was not then printed—barring two or three of the last verses. The occasion of it was an intolerably cold, wet, and evil year for farmers, whom he deeply commiserated, and whom he longed to re-inspire with hope and to incite to fresh efforts by his brilliant " forecasts " of a bright time coming.

The brother of this remarkable man was also a mechanical genius in his way, and an ardent amateur musician, and I once had in my hands a beautiful fiddle he had made with his knife solely out of a portion of a paling rail taken from a gap in a thorn hedge. Both brothers have now " joined the majority," leaving no sign, and for some time I have lost all trace of the whereabouts of their surviving relatives. I print again the full rhyme in order to illustrate and record the indefatigable industry, ingenuity, and, I may add, the admirable sagacity of this wonderful being.

"THE WAUTHER."

" Auld Lees' " been tichtly exerceesed this while about the
    " wauther,"
That endless theme to ferm folk ó' deevilish frait and
    bather ;

K

Sae in my noddle a' his pranks hae been conspiring lang,
To mak' me sit an' ease mysel' wi' a bit blast o' sang.

He kens a' kinds barometers—the *Siphon* ; *Common Wheel ;*
The *Hermatic*—" puir man's wauther gless "—that never
    does work weel ;
The touchy *Sympiesometer*, of heedrogen an' ile ;
An' mony a sic-like instrument—owre fashious here to style.

Leeze me on his thermometers that tell o' cauld an' heat—
Hoo muckle or hoo little aye will gar ane grue or sweat ;
Or, wi' a meenit's feegurin', as owre the hills we stride,
Can tell 's their hichts, maist to an inch, abune the Norlan
    Tide.

Rain gauges, spheres to weigh the winds, an' note hoo fast
    they blaw,
Anemometers, Hygrometers, Electrometers braw,
Maps, plates, an' grit charts synchronous o' storms past an'
    to come,
An' learn'd gab ambiguous, their grand results to sum !

He'll state hoo great the pressure is owre sich a wide
    areeay,
As Europe or America—as 'twere his ain idea ;
And, wi' a visage grave as Job's, tell whaur at " 4 p.m.
The lift was blue, the sea was smooth, an' a'thing else the
    same."

" Winds are the ae deerect result o' change o' temp'rature,
Whan air is hett it rises, like the steam o' toddy pure ;
Syne in to fill the vawcum sweep the gusts off every neuk,
Just like oor hens at feedin' time when Ailie cries ' chuck,
    chuck !' "

Thus tells he in a jiffy the cause o' every storm,
But what's the cause o' *that* cause, alack ! wha can inform ?
Here Lees' "profoondly ignorant," an' claws his head and
  says—
"The Wauther Clerk caps Beaconsfield in 's unexpected
  ways !

"The currents aikquatorial an' polar rise an' fa',
But why they dae sae, at sich times, I canna find ava !
Before I e'en can *guess* that Why, far far'er maun I peer—
But I do trow the truth lies in the Northern Hemisphere !

"This year has had a surfeit o' the tempests o' the warld—
Canadian frosts an' Polar snaws roond 's infant thrapple
  swirl'd ;
Syne *Monsoons, Simoons, Tornadoes,* an' *Levanters* frae the
  east,
Wi' *Boreal* squalls 'tween coorses, have comprised his constant feast.

"Then mists, an' rain in deluges, have drouk't an' drench'd
  him weel ;
Pestiferous, deleterious blasts have pierced his bouk like
  steel ;
Disastrous caulds an' arid gales have brocht him pain an'
  blicht—
Till noo, like drugg'd incurable, he'd fain succumb outricht !

"Puir deevils are the farmers a' ! My heart loups to my
  mou'
To hear them murn their sad, sad lot—nae gleam o' hope
  shines through !

But they maun dicht their tears amain an' look Fate in the
    face,
An' daur her warst like Scottishmen—to whom despair's
    disgrace.

" Let ' Almanacks ' an' ' Wauther Seers ' foretell o' ' evil
    days !'—
Vile caterers to ignorance—wha lie because it pays !
Pass them a' by as knavish rants—nane scans the Wauther
    gleam
Beyond twa days for certain—hoosoever wise they seem !

" Neither be o' hope forlorn, but frae this deid wa' o' time
Streetch to pluck the golden fruitage, peerin' surely thro'
    its grime.
There are lessons hung like signboards, that a little child
    may read,
What your wants are—how to fill them—tho' Necessity
    cry *speed !*

" Then the mirk hour o' the present in immediate time
    shall be
The prelude, birth, an' earnest o' retored prosperity.
The overthrow o' Poortith grim maun aye forerun the reign
O' the smiling prince his brither--jovial Plenty, fat and
    fain !"

PROFESSOR BLACKIE ON CONFESSIONS
OF FAITH.

—:—

NDER the heading of "Creeds and Canaries" there appeared some very clever lines by the late professor of the Greek Chair in the University of Edinburgh. Notwithstanding, I do not agree with their author upon the subject so deftly and neatly disposed of in them—to wit, the "mooring" of the intellectual life and theological beliefs of Christian ministers in this advanced age to a fallible document propounded and drawn up by a body of fallible and comparatively ignorant men upwards of two centuries ago. Hence the following rhyme by way of answer to him.

LARKS AND LIBERTY.

I had a little laverock bird
Whose doleful song was scarcely heard
   The gilded cage beyond it ;
All day it leapt from perch to perch
As if for freedom sweet in search !
Day after day—again, again—
It tried and tried, but all in vain—
   Its jail securely bound it !

One morn the glorious summer sun,
To gladden nature wide, begun
   His upwards march thro' Heaven,

In love and joyous liberty
The larks, like *Blackies*, sang on high ;
" Poor bird," I said, and op'ed the door,
" Come out and join the merry core—
    Come out, release is given ! "

Down from the topmost spar it leapt,
Whisk ! thro' the door ajar it swept
    As hawk-death were behind it !
Then up the sparkling morning air—
Up, up it mounted, singing rare,
In grateful raptures and elate,
A lay to Freedom consecrate,
    That now no cage did bind it !

" If birds are wise, men are not fools ! "
For they, too, hate their narrow rules
    And old dogmatic cages !
" And should you wish to make them free,
Just ope the door and you will see "
How all agog, with plumed wing,
They ready are to soar and sing
    With Truth's own bards and sages !

" The lawyer and the grave D.D.,"
Whom sect-dividing enmity
    In life-long strife engages,
Might then fling to the winds their " creeds,"
And cease to fight schismatic screeds,
And turn to preach and practise free
At last *True Christianity*,
    Which knows no " gilded cages ! '

ANE DEEVLISH PRANK OF YE
WICKED ELFIN KING.

—:—

FAR up the glen, on a whinny knowe,
    Yellow-haired Effie sat a' day,
Plaitin' a snood for her dreamy brow,
  An' learnin' the lintie's sweet, sweet lay,
    Till the gloamin' fell
    O'er the lonely dell ;
Oh, bonnie Effie, gae hame, gae hame—
    Thy minnie'll froon
    An' ye come na soon,
An' auld angirt faither do mair than blame.

"Gude nicht, lintie, I'm aff an' awa ;
  Gude nicht, burnie, too ;
An' a wee, wee kiss for my wee flowers a',
  The fairest that ever grew !
    Oh ! just like a bee,
    Am I happy wi' thee,
As I sing thro' the lang simmer day,
    Wi' the sun-blinks coming,
    Where the bees are humming
Lilts o' true Nature, the lealest for aye !"

Foxgloves, bluebells, thimmels, an' spinks,
  Lootit their heids a-wee ;
She gazit doon the glen where the burnie jinks,
  Ane waesome wench to see ;

"O the stars are shootin',
An' the kye are routin',
An' hame I maun gang, ye weel, weel ken ;
I'll come agen
To this bonnie glen,
An' luve ye for leavin' ye a' nicht alane !"

Noo, a blae wee deevilick Son o' an Elf,
Was crooned the king o' his tribe,
Had heard a' this, and quo' he to himself—
Wi' ouphish like lauch an' jibe—
"Eicht queens are mine,
She'll make the nine ;
O stars ! O stars ! by the moon woo'd well,
We'se caper an' sing,
We'se dance in a ring,
Wi' the king i' the middle—mysel', mysel' !"

He pressit his horn to his impish mou'
An' toutit three times three ;
Like bells his twa cheeks were blawn, I trow,
An' the tears ran frae his e'e.
"Rat-a-too ! rat-a-too !"
He summoned his crew
Wi' an elfin blast under the mune,
They heard the command—
In the clap o' a hand
They were swarming below an' abune.

Wee Effie, sac mazed, she sank on the swaird,
In a leefu' an' sleepy-like dwam ;
The king o' the Elves, a snell proud caird,
Spake orders to bind the wee lamb !

" And carry," said he,
" Her tenderlie
All unto my palace so fine ;
For there in Elfland,
In the silk so grand,
Of my queens she'll be queen o' the nine ! "

Up the glen in the moonshine, awa, awa,
Wi' vólte, an' caper, an' funk,
They danced, they snappit, an' heuched awa,
Like Alloway's ghaists a' drunk.
An' the valley a' rang,
As the burnie sang—
" O Effie, wee Effie, fareweel, fareweel !
Lang years three times three
Elf queen ye maun be,
An' sigh for auld Garvie in revel an' reel ! "

MORHAM DELL.*

[FOUNDED ON AN ACTUAL DREAM.]

—:—

WHAN Nicht had closèd the Day's ae e'e,
    A-watchin' the yowes, sleep found out me !
An' I laid me doun on the clover-land,
Like wrack on an unkenn'd ocean strand.
"Sweet Morham Dell ! sweet Morham Dell !
Fairies an' moonshine love thee well,"
Sang a wee voice as there I lay—
An' again unto me its winsome way :—
" Sleep no more, dream no more—hearken to me !
Fair Queen Mab, 'neath ane rowan tree,
Low, low lies in pale sickness laid ;
We go to bring her Leech with our cavalcade."
Then up sough'd a night wind, strong an' shrill,
To waft me athort yon eerie hill—
Whare Auld Garvie bursts its broken way
Doun Snawdon's lanely Howe astray.
I thocht o' the Leech as on I sped—
Ane auld Warlock, gray and staid,
Wha wins by himsel' in a rocky cave,
Whilk, when he dies, will be his grave.
In an eerie den between twa linns
O' the Garvie, this warlock wins—

---

* A beautiful little glen, about a mile and a half west from Traprain
Law, noted for its fairies, in the poetic "days of Eld."

Bearded an' rough—of antique line—
On 's shoonless shins, three feet an' nine.

 " O warlock o' the Snawdon Howe ! "
   The elfins cried,
 "'Leech o' the fairies—ever thou,
   Trusty and tried ;
Haste thee, haste thee, Warlock, haste !
Steer up, pack up pottle and paste,
Low, low, on the swaird o' Morham Dale
Lies our Lady stricken an' pale.
  O haste !
Convoy and all is ready and made
For thee in our royal cavalcade !
  Let bugles blow ! "

  * * * * *

First, then, in the multitude
Rode the grave Leech in high mood ;
Then a fairy maiden came,
In white locks of elfin fame—
Pure of heart, tho' queen-like—she
Driving in her coach an' three.
By her side of royal mien,
Consort o' the sickly queen
Rode an Afric Cat—whose eyes
Burn'd like stars in frosty skies.
Then lo ! the musicianers—
Mab ! a glorious band is hers—
Horn on high, so sweet and clear,
Starnies droopt half way to hear.
They play'd ane fairy burial pæan,
Till old Night did sigh again ;

Then an imp-like, ouphish ditty,
Made the vera Leech grow witty.
        I leuch—
For the very air did quiver
Round them, over them, and ever,
Till they a' passed but Ane, and he
Dash'd his fire-tail in mine e'e !
" Therefore ! " quo he, an' flew on,
Leaving me to grieve an' groan :—
O'er me stoopt ('twas a' in sleep),
An' smellit my face—my Southdown Sheep !

OUR AIN WEE TOUN.

[HADDINGTON.]

—:—

OH, dizens are the cities I've parawded up an' doun,
    But fient a ane's comparable to auld Ada's toun!
There's Glesca? smoor'd wi' reek! There's Lon'on? over-
    grown!
They canna haud a caunle to OUR AIN WEE TOUN!

Throo foreign lands I've rammlet, and mony touns I've
    seen—
Wi' "capitols" and "avenues," and big kirks in between:
Wi' streets a' made like railways, whaur cars ran up an'
    doun,
But the *Lang Cause'ay* cowes them a' in OUR WEE TOUN!

The black folk an' the Hielanders have houses in the hills—
The feck are rabbit warrens, an' the lave are whisky stills—
An' thae they ca' their "Tounships," in whilk folk aften
    drown,
Like to kittlins in the *Lang Cram* at OUR WEE TOUN!

In Embro' they hae biggins on the vera Calton's broo,
In the Cowgate there are dwellings that wad sicken ev'n a
    soo!
They hae tours an' michty lang lums, an' a Castle for a
    croun,
But they haena gat a *Steeple* like OUR AIN WEE TOUN!

The auld toun—Our Ain Toun—is beautiful an' fine ;
She is the Queen o' a' touns on Tiber, Thames, or Tyne !
What toun can boast a *John Knox* or a *Commentator
  Brown ?*
Or a bardie like the *Samuel* o' OUR WEE TOUN ?

Nane o' them has a Nungate—far less a Nungate Brig !
"Sautmarkets," an' "Broomielaws " in prent look vera
  big ;
But you'll agree wi' me my freen' whan yince ye've view'd
  them roun',
By far the most remarkable is OUR WEE TOUN !

Wastminster an' muckle Paul's are nae doubt unco kirks,
The Roman an' the Yorkshire anes are fairish mason warks ;
But a stap ye maun gang far'er, tho' ye tramp a' Earth
  aroun',
Ere ye match the *Lamp o' Lothian* o' OUR AIN WEE TOUN.

Syne as for " splendid moniments !"   Whare-ever can there
  be
Sic famous fanes as our fanes, at hame or owre the sea ?
The Knox, the Home, the Tweeddale, forbye lots knockit
  doun,
Declare for sculpts maist marvellous is OUR WEE TOUN !

Nor less renown'd for living folk than for stookies o' the
  deid,
Our Wee Toun's wally offspring in life's race tak' the lead :
Frae the highest to the lowest—frae the Provost in his
  goun,
To the street waif in his tatters, far in front shutes OUR
  WEE TOUN !

For lawyers, scribes, an' ministers we surely bear the gree,
We hae sae mony o' them that few ither folk we see !
To Courts an' Kirks they jostle like to drive ilk ither doun,
'Twere best to leave them to themselves in OUR WEE TOUN.

"THE DAFT DAYS."

—:—

WHEN abune our Loudon plain,
  Like King Winter on his throne,
Tower'd the muckle Law Traprain,
  Wi' a snawy mantle on,
And his heid wreath'd wi' mist for a croun,
  Cam' the Daflin Days again—
  Rowthy Yule and a' his train,
  Bearing glorious cheer amain
        To our toun !

Let ajar the schule doors flee,
  And like sheep frae out the fauld
Mark the youngsters burst in glee,
  Lads and lasses bricht and bauld,
Hurrahing for the " New Year Holiday ! "
  Books and slates owre shouthers swung,
  What a yelping mak' the young !—
  Happy heart mak's tattling tongue,
        Nicht and day !

Hame belyve. But from that hour,
  Till the schule gaes in again,
Mithers ! dream of Peace no more,
  But give Hubbub room and rein,
To exhibit his mad frolicing galore !
  Busk the brats in droll array,

Guiserding they a' maun gae—
Guiserding for "Hogmanay,"
      Door to door !

New Year's morn, "first-footing" owre,
  In to Embro' some will flee ;
Some alang gun-barrels glower,
  Aiming at a far "bull's e'e, '
And loudly silence pierce the lee-lang day !
  Twa-three on their sins will pore,
  Crowds in Publics haud the splore,
  And, be-muddled, brawl and roar,
      Yea or nay !

But the same—the same auld sky,
  Shade and sunshine meet and mix ;
Just as ither years gane by,
  Comes this pilgrim Ninety-Six,
A pack upon his back of fate for a' !
  Tramp, tramp, tramp alang his route,
  Day by day, he'll count us out
  Life and death, and change to boot,
      Grit and sma' !

Tragedy and comedy,
  Drama, drivel—what he will,
On this earth stage, scores per day,
  He'll "bring out" and act wi' skill,
Shifting the scenes wi' god-like art and speed ;
  Men, the puppets of his play ;
  "Kings" or "subjects," sons of clay,
  Thousands on their backs he'll lay,
      Stiff and deid !

L

Sae time, year by year, rolls on
    As it 's been sae will it be
But tho' millions thus have flown
    Hastens, Bardie, sune to thee—
A *black* ane, that thy " rhymes " will quaten a' !
    But ne'er moonge, man, sing it through
Yarns mak not—if joys are—few !
    Ever, whilst thou wag'st thy pow,
        Rhyme awa' !

OUR JOHNNIE.

—:—

HO ! here he comes again wi' his Shanter capie on,
    An' buskit an' dinkit like a Prince Royal !
Upo' his Mammy's knee at nicht he rules as on a throne,
  An' young an' auld within the house are his subjects loyal!
      Haith ! for a fowre year auld,
      He is a Ruler bauld !
A Tyrant an' a Despot wha will never brook denial !

He awaukens i' the morning by first scriech o' day,
    Screamin' like a corbie for " something to eat !"
An' his " Mammy " jumps up, withouten delay ;
    For, oh, her " Bonnie Darling she hates to hear greet !"
      Sae he rairs an' he clatters—
      What cares he for his betters,
Loud yelping at five o'clock for " something to eat ?"

The women-folk o' the house he rules like his slaves,
    Wha daurna for their vera lives his word disobey ;
For instant comes the penalty gin ane misbehaves,
    In yells waur than Grumphie's on the killin' day !
      Wi' his face thrawn out o' shape,
      An' his little mou' agape,
Most unyirthly skirls he metes them wha daur his will
    gainsay !

Dabblin' in a glaur-hole, or wading i' the burn,
    This Despot in a daidley aft passes an hour ;

Or, captain o' the bairn band, he tak's the foremost " turn "
  Swingin' on the gairden gate or plout'rin' i' the stour.
        Hoo weel he does subdue 'em !
        Hoo laigh they a' bow to him !
Ha ! his threat that he'll " tell Mammy " gars the bauldest
  o' them coo'r !

When comes his early bed-time, an' he's deid tired at last,
  Our Monarch abdicates, an' is pleased a bairn to be ;
Then aff come little booties, little socks, an' coaties fast,
  An' doun in his wee nicht-gown he slips at Mammy's
  knee !
        There wi' faulded hands he kneels,
        And in innocence appeals,
To Him wha of the children said—" Suffer them to come to
  Me ! "

What wonder is it then if a tender woman doats,
  On a brawny bairn like this, an' is blind to ev'ry faut ?
Let her wair her love upon him—time will rub out mony
  blots !
But the true love o' his Mother, it shall never come to
  naught !
        Doun to his latest day
        It will licht life's chequered way,
And illume wi' ray divine Sorrow's dreariest, darkest spat !

ON HEARING THE RESULT OF THE
HADDINGTON BURGHS' ELECTION OF 1878.

—:—

$\mathcal{A}$LAS, alas ! beyond hope, "done !"
 Vain now, Sir James, our roaring fun,
And kissing fisher carlins !
Yon Jethart lads may snap the thoom,
And sweer the farce had its fit doom
 In you smack o' Macfarlane's !

O for a shaird o' Watty's wit
To shrine in deathless verse each cit
 That rallied round our banners ;
To tell wha focht, an' tell wha bled,
What turncoats wheel'd, an' cowards fled,
 What true men pluck'd fresh honours !

Thee, U. P. Robson—first afield—
" Free born !" an' " born," too, to wield
 The club iconoclastic !
Thy fell onslauchts wha didna rin—
As did Sir Jamie—a' but *ane !*
 Thon dread ecclesiastic !

A " seer," yecleped " St Martin bauld,"
Next for that kirk that's ca'd " The Auld "
 Renounced his quondam allies ;
An' would have swept them from the field,
Had they but let, or he been skill'd
 In that trade like Auld Wallace !

Him smash'd—neist see " The Councillor "
Of Jethart come the ranks before
    And fling his gauntlet, crying—
"Fair play ! fair play ! "   Then, ere ye'd wink,
Sir James this knight unhorsed—some think
    By babbin' down, or shying !

Then " Ketchen " fierce to the rescue
His " floorers " from a wallet drew,
    An' hurl'd them at the Tory !
As Neptune's spurn'd by St Abb's rock,
The Baronet repell'd the shock,
    An' glitter'd with new glory !

But see—oh see !--yon priest arise,
With foaming mouth an' wat'ry eyes,
    His former faith denying :
Roaring—" I 'scaped from War's fire school,
Even Afric and Sebastapol,"
    The *canaille rout* defying !

Perforce the Liberal hosts shall quake
When this mad turncoat for kirk's sake
    Baas like a bull before 'em ?
Alas for Fury, tried full sore,
The more he roar'd, they roar'd still more,
    Till dumb as death they wore him !

Now in the lists rode forth a " chield "
With " Nungate ! " blazon'd on his shield,
    Which guid deeds aft had burnish'd ;
But tho' a soger tried an' true,
Even him Sir James quite " overthrew "—
    With lance a friend had furnish'd !

Oh, rare to see the fence between
The veteran warrior an' the green
 When close the last was corner'd !
Be praised ! a " Ragman," and a carle
Ca'd " Gemmell," snatchit frae the parle
 The Chief—just as he founder'd !

Another joust ! another knight—
In fact, a *pair*—prolong'd the fight,
 An' kept a' Scotland grinning !
Calvert an' Sprott within the ring,
Twa Blackcoat braves, engaged full swing,
 An' sent ilk ither spinning !

At last the greatest o' them a'—
The Dunbar Ajax, by whase ca'
 An' Ulysses-like schemin',
Himsel' comes marching owre the plain,
Leading his subject fisher train
 An' randy fisher women !

Tears gratefu' gleam'd in Sir J.'s e'e
His true-blue following a' to see
 Where he is " known so finely ! "
Oh, gallant wax'd his knightly heart,
Ae " half-daft " wife he drew apart,
 An' kiss'd her " just divinely ! "

Then Ajax spak' the meed of war—
Writ by himsel'—to suit Dunbar—
 In simple terms an' candid :—
" *For victory, we shall leave alane*
The Auld Kirk to the tapmaist stane,
 An' fix the Harbour splendid ! "

Alas ! alas ! even this was vain !
The gathering nicht closed doun amain,
    An' black defeat brak' o'er them !
So closed this far-famed Waponschaw,
But neist time they their claymore's draw,
    Anither tale 's before them !

MARRIAGE LINES.

[WRITTEN AT THE CELEBRATION OF THE HAPPY NUPTIALS O'

MR SANDY SELLAR AND MISS AILIE LOWRIE.*]

—:—

NOW bauld March shrilly blaws his horn
To trumpet in the spring's return,
An' gi'es the train o' winter, passed
Out owre the north, a parting blast.
The farmer hears his warnin' ca',
And casts the seed in faith awa'.
The wild flowers feel his subtle breath,
And wake, and smile at winter's wrath ;
The daisy, and meek vi'let even,
Dare the chill blast, and spread to heaven
Their shiv'ring banners, whilk foretell
Sweet spring's approach to down and dell.

And nature animate as weel
His rousing influence doth feel ;
The lambkins owre the greening braes
In frolic mood begin their plays.
The laverock mounts to heaven's gate
To lilt his love for his new mate ;

---

* "Sandy Sellar" is a master mechanic on the shady side of life—
considerably. His excellent bride—not so young either—is the daughter
of a well-known Lothian farmer. The story goes in the neighbourhood
that "Sandy" courted for upwards of twenty years before he summoned
pluck to "pop the question." But he succeeded for all that !

The coupled paitricks "scriech at e'en,"
The sparrows chirp the showers between.

Fu' sune they'll flee, lang straes in mou'
Wi' love an' nests richt thrang, I trew ;
And mated mawkins owre the fiel'
Whid after ither, rear, an' wheel,
The lee-lang day ; the rabbits even
An extra share o' spunk are given— .
Alang the plantin' sides they bicker,
An' funk up their white fuddies quicker,
Or munch an' map, an' stamp their paws
Wi' gusto equal to its cause ;
While mavis clear, and blackie-bird,
Doun Tyne's sweet valley blythe are heard !

Such being the micht o' March's power
O'er bird an' beast, an' tree an' flower,
What wonder then, if Nature's lord,
Even Man himsel', should feel restored,
And something of the general heat
In his thaw'd breast begin to friet !
In sooth, this natural feeling, vast
An' strange, ower heart o' Sandy pass'd,
Ae nicht as sighing he drew near
The weel kenn'd dwelling o' his dear.

Quo' he, " I've been a wanter lang—
This nicht maun change or end my sang,
For I shall strecht the ' question ' pop,
And, from her lips, despair or hope
Shall seal my fate an' stap my fear ;
This nicht—this vera nicht—I swear ! "

Sae strechtway, then, he order'd Johnie
To gang direck and yoke the pownie,
Whilk, buckled to, awa' they drive
Wi' cauld wind an' het love to strive,
Freezing an' burning, out an' in,
The lang five miles they had to rin ;
But Sandy, pondering the while
His manly errand, and the style
That he'd adopt wi' his dear jo,
Was stone dead to all else below.

" Bed-fast auld mither lies," thocht he,
" Whate'er her ailing it may be,
Sae I'll fetch yont my Sweet to see her,
Syne what I may I can do wi' her ;
And, aince for a', as I'm a man—
Ask her to be my wife aff-han' ! "

The plot, thus deeply schemed, an' laid
In rich fulfilment soon was made
A grand success. That Friday week
His now " gude-faither " he did seek,
And tauld him hoo an' what he meant,
And, " Oh ! wad he gie his consent ? "
The auld man fidged, syne blunt his mind
He spak' richt howe, yet plain an' kind—
"This month," says he, "'s the month o' Mairch—
An unco month for wives to sairch,
But, shure as Mairch love's wind does blaw,
My full consent—ye hae it a',
Tak' her, my lad, an' mak' her thine—
Ye'se ne'er reproach the day ye twine
Wi' Ailie in the marriage knot,

But ca't the pearl o' life's lot ;
For, tho' she's dootless younger been,
As you, yoursel', my ancient frien',
She is a lass weel worth the honour,
By splicing wi' her ye'd put on her;
She's been reared weel up to the mark,
She kens the nobleness o' wark.
'Twas wark that made me what I am,
And she her wark will never sham.
To mak' a sark, or wash ain either,
My faigs, she winna hang or swither.
In culinary maitters, too,
She's great at kail and tatty-broo ;
Or genty things, like pancakes good,
Or stews, or crowdy—wale o' food !
Or even bread trashtrie for a bairn,
Or bileing eggs, or frying herrin'—
Tak' tent o' me, my word rely on,
Her skeel in a' there's nae doun-cryin'.
She's sich a mistress o' the airt,
She kens the cookery book by hairt.
As shure my son-in-law to be,
As she ane precious bairn to me
Has ever been, as shure your haine
An' your board end she winna shame.
She's nane o' your Miss Modern schule,
Unfit for spence or kitchen rule—
But a douce, mensefu' weel-faur'd queen,
Can grace the hame hersel' keeps clean ;
With head an' hairt sae stock'd to be
Her lord's fit fallow, full an' free ;
An' can o' nights, out-owre her seam,
Maintain her side, whate'er the theme,

Be't war, the kirk, or politics,
Or scand'lous, breach o' promise tricks,
Or craps, or markets, shares, or books—
The latest novel, or the fooks
O' the last mode, brent new frae Paris,
Contrived by Worth to deck the dearies ;
Thairfore, my son, and to conclude,"
The auld man closed in sober mood,
" Tak' her at aince, and my consent
Have wi' her, without grudge or stint,
For tho' I'm laith to lose her noo
My loss, dear friend, is gain to you !"

Awa' ran Sandy, and fell sune
The news was trockit thro' the toun ;
Rumour, as usual, loused her packs,
And barter'd guesses in a' cracks ;
Tho' naething but this truth was there,
The golden fact—they'd mak' a pair.

Sae tailors, claes, an' mantua makers,
Pigmen, an' grocer folk, an' bakers,
Were on the rump o' business ridin',
Wi' orders for the grand " Providin'."

Wow, what a hubbub then was seen,
The house was turn't frae morn to e'en,
Intil a show, bazaar, and fair,
Wi' bedding, chairs, an' crockery ware,
An' bundles, bales, bend boxes, barrels,
Eneuch to mak' ane think this warl's
Owre sair misjudged, owre sair maligned,
For sure, when siccan walth's designed,

For only twa, it scarce can be,
That some 's sae steeped in misery.
Howe'er, 'mang turmoil, stir, an' roarin',
The great auspicious hour wore on ;
As day by day the bride grew leaner,
And day by day the bridegroom keener.

His circulation running wild,
He grew as restless as a child ;
Nor sleep nor rest for nichts had he,
And, oh, but he sighed piteously ;
His haill heart being wi' her he loved,
He thocht the eicht-day clock ne'er moved ;
An' round and round, an' up an' doun,
He scour'd a' corners o' the toun ;
Discarding even his urbane manners,
An' blawing like our auld mill fanners.
A raving wretch at lairge ran he,
Ane fearsome " spectacle " to see,
Wham neither sneesh nor dram braucht ease,
But only made him bock an' sneeze.
At length—the fates be praised an' thankit !—
Auld time doun to this nicht has shankit ;
An' lang an' last, bridegroom an' bride,
Are leash'd by Hymen side by side !

As new life opens to the twain,
May it bring peace to either ane ;
Syne, screivin' doun to auld age gang,   .
As rowth an' happy as it's lang.
May cheerfu' plenty boil their pat,
An' greedy health say grace to that ;
While truthfu' love's ain pledges dear,

The girning bairnies fast appear ;
And till thae bairnies' bairns flock,
A guid tribe round the parent stock,
Mak' their hame thine—thou glorious three—
Peace, pleasure, and prosperity !

THE WEE BROUN SQUIRREL.

[A GREENWOOD RHYME.]

—:—

IN the fir plantin', frae the screich o' day,
　　Like the plumed prince o' the greenwood warl'
What time the elfins daurna shake a tae—
　　Up a tree, look at me, the wee broun squirrel !
　　　　Merrier than cuckoo heard,
　　　　Gleger than swallow bird,
"Puck" himsel's a gowk to me—a wee broun squirrel.

Deep in the heart o' the evergreen tree,
　　Far frae the ken o' the muneshine crew,
Rockit by the winds my forest bowers be,
　　The cushat's my trumpeter—croodle, croodle, doo !
　　　　Gyte wi' luve—railin',
　　　　Cooin', an' wailin',
Simmer nicht an' mornin' croodle, croodle, doo !

Swith as the hoolet to's auld blichtit tree,
　　Stealeth on saft wing at early cock-craw,
Bright as a star flaucht, I spoot up on hie,
　　What time the laverocks on morn's star ca'—
　　　　Cockit luggies, curly
　　　　Lang tail, an' swirly,
Twinklin' on the lerrick taps in the wauk'nin' daw !

The born Jack-tar o' the woodland am I—
"Steeple-Jack" daurna wage a spiel wi' me !
Yon spruce-pine tap, spearin' the howe sky,
   I wad lay it at his feet or he'd coont three !
        Up, like the hawk, I'd vault,
        Down, like the thunderbolt,
Syne, oh whaur, " Steeple-Jackie," wad a' yer glory be ?

Up a tree, look at me, the wee broun squirrel,
   Merrier than Robin Hood, the lea-lang day !
Ye little plumed prince o' the greenwood warl'
   What time the nicht fays daurna shake a tae,
        Cockit lugs, an' curly
        Lang tail, an' swirly,
A' the elves are sloths to me, the wee broun squirrel !

IN THE AULD KIRKYARD.

—:—

'N a sunny, genial day,
　　When at length the mid-aged May
Wi' the braird begude to busk the waukenin' earth in
green,
　　I teuk my staff in hand,
　　And, sudden, slipped the band
Whilk hauds us to the warld roond a stake o' troubles
keen !

　　Tho' wyled by mony a flower,
　　I stayed-na ance to glour,
Till the siller-gleaming Tyne sang her pæans at my feet !
　　Then,—like the bard I felt
　　In my freedom fond—I knelt
At the shrine o' Nature, spell-bound wi' her look sae fair
an' sweet !

　　A' doun the sheltered haughs,
　　The towering feathery saughs,
Like queens august waved welcomes to the realms o' wood
an' stream ;
　　'Neath their fairy-flickering shade,
　　Ane enchanted wight I strayed,
Wi' the "banks an' braes" around me—in a rapt Elysian
dream !

　　On an' on, thro' yellow broom,
　　Birks an hawthorns, briars in bloom,

Cowslips full flowered, springing brackens, daffodils ;
    Linties singing simmer's theme,
    To the deep-pleased, lingering stream—
Zephyrs fragrant, roaming idly o'er the hills.

    Past the mill an' the green wood,
    Whaur a leafless rowan stood,
Like the wraith o' distraught winter—still unlaid
    Ere I wist, mysel' I found
    In the kirkyaird's waukrife bound—
Waking up to conscious being, whaur soun' sleep th'
    unconscious dead !

    Thro' a winnock, left undraped,
    O' the lonely kirk I peep'd—
It was empty, silent, vasty, eerie, weird ;
    Sic an awesomeness within,
    That a running mousie's din
Wad gart ane start an' shudder as a skulking ghaist he
    heard !

    But the golden gloaming blazed,
    And.my fancy, as I gazed,
Restored the shadowy temple and worshippers of yore !
    I heard auld James "invoke,"
    There stood our aulk-kent folk,
In reverent postures lowly—as they stood in life before !

    Tears, burning, scorched my e'en
    As I fond recalled each frien',
Whyles I tholed the dread fact waefu'—" In their graves
    they sleep aroun' ! "

Sae I turn'd, in sorrow fain,
The auld names to con again—
That affection, lonely sighing, on memorial stane hath
hewn !

Somehow, our footsteps creep
Aye whaur our ain kin sleep ;
Sae, by rote, I haply saunter'd near a weel-kenned auld ash
tree !
On a sair jee'd, moss-grown stane,
Lang I leaned an' made my mane
For that far-back age—the golden—when my warld was
mother's knee !

For her ! her " laddie's " tears,
Some twenty cauldrife years,
Have well'd an' flow'd, an' dried ; and well'd an' flow'd
again !
Wi' some sma' blinks between,
Sae stormy life has been—
That aft her laddie's bark shored to strew wi' wrack the
main !

But thro' a' those years to him
(As the Heaven-lit pole star's beam),
The memory o' a mother's love hath beacon'd every shoal !
Let seas with tempests war—
Ae rift may serve a star,
To ward the seaman lonely to his love-encompass'd goal !

Fareweel, thou sacred dust-
Safe garner'd in His trust !—
Hope pierces the dark shadow with a golden beam of Day !

Shine on, O Beam divine !
Wi' glowing lustre shine !
As we draw the " bourne " nearer—making light death's
dreary way !

TESTIMONIALS TO PROVOSTS.

[A DREAM.]

—:—

WHEN I had read the ell lang list
   O' names o' them wha did persist
To gi'e a gift to Brodie,*
I slippit canny aff to bed,
An' fell a dov'rin'—sair bestead,
   An' rack'd in mind an' body ;
I didna mind the " uncos " lang
   That Friday night, I trew !
" Births, Marriages, an' Deaths "—an' "sangs "
An' " jokes " (a motley crew !)
Gaed whummlin' an' jummlin'
   In riot thro' my brain,
Till sound sleep did me steep
   In Lethè's stream again.

But faigs ! nae mair than ance or twice
I hadna snored, whan, in a trice,
   An' distinck in a dream,
An ancient carle before me rose,
Whase features—tousie heid, an' nose—
   'Maist like mine ain did seem.
Quoth he—" Son ' Sam !' tak' ye nae fricht,
   In faith look me upon ;
I'm come wi' you to crack this nicht—
   Hear me, my Famous Son !

---

* The well-known and much respected ex-Provost of North Berwick.

Auld Dawvid, yon braw lad,*
Lies sair upo' my heart—
To wham ye nae gift gi'e
    For a' his great desairt.

" Roose up, my son, let fly thy wit—
The curst disgrace nail to the bit
    Till Loudon girns for shame ; ⁻
Tell o' his great warks 'mang the drains—†
Tell o' his superhuman pains
    To bring the water hame.
That caller water, saft and clear—
That priceless Chesters Water !
Whilk than sour swipes or ' table beer,'
    Is, oh ! sae muckle better !
Sae sure aye, sae pure aye,
    In coggie, caup, or tin ;
To cook wi', or douk wi',
    Or wash the workman's skin !

" That water triumph, tell them, ' Sam,'
A greater was than ony sham
    Won on the battle-field—
Napoleon, Lord of Austerlitz,
Nay, Dunbar Brand, wi' a' his wits,
    To such a feat maun yield.‡
At their high best, what did they do
But tap puir human bluid ?

---

* The late David Stevenson, Esq., Provost of Haddington. Mr
Stevenson was presented with his portrait.

† He was the leader of the party who ultimately succeeded in efficiently
draining and bringing a supply of water into the " Auld Toun."

‡ A pleasantry which is no longer applicable. Dunbar has now a new
and full supply of pure water.

But Dawvid tapt a stream, I trew,
    That flows for nocht but guid,
Life-giving, reviving
    The weary mortal man,
And watering, and scattering
    Wealth, health on every han'!

"But when ye thro' the past hae run,
Mind Dawvid. 'Sam,' o' wark undone—
    The Railway and the Gas ;*
The Schules, likewise, micht better be ;
The Streets—the Streets are waur to see
    Than Killiecrankie Pass.
Whan ye gang to the guid auld toun
    Wi' tatties cheap an' fine,
I'm aft deid feart that ye'll clash doun,
    An' row strecht into Tyne ;
The knowes there, the howes there,
    As ye drive ower yer cairt,
Do fret me an' threat me
    Your teeth an' jaws to pairt !

"And last, but not the least, my son—
The chief o' a' that's left undone—
    A New Brig ower the Tyne,†
The Nungate ane—the shame o' Cairns—
For dougs may do fu' weel—or bairns,
    Their bits o' 'cairts' to twine.
But wow, its back is hump'd wi' age,
    It mocks what it adorns ;
Ev'n Robb, your Antiquarian Sage,
    Its rainbow passage scorns.

---

* Two other long spoken of schemes.
† A fondly cherished project ; but one, alas, which is not even initiated yet.

Get throo then a new ane,
    And in the by-and-bye
The auld ane can hald then
    The cla'es hung out to dry.

" And noo, aboot the gift ye'll gie :
Son 'Sam,' appropriate it should be,
    And worthy o' the man !
His pictyoor ? Pooh ; he kens himsel'
He is your Local Gladstone Swell !
    What then ? My lad, aff haun—
Gi'e him a bath. Then he may dip,
    An' douk an' drench him weel.
At hame in that fine liquid sip
    He brocht from far a-fiel' :
'Twill lichten and brichten,
    As weel as plumps in Tyne ;
And clean him, and sheen him,
    The mair an' mair to shine.

" Fareweel, my son ; my time is up ;
Ye ken that speerits daurna clip
    An hour frae aff the morn ;
But at the first craw o' the cock
Aff we maun pack, like tod or brock,
    To our dark mystic bourne.
Ta-ta ! I'll see ye sune again."
    He waved his hand and fled ;
I turn'd mysel' an' ope'd my een,
    Syne bounced strecht up in bed ;
How, Lord ! then, I roar'd then,
    An' fair wi' mirth did scream ;
An' cough'd lang, and laugh'd lang,
    To fin' 'twas a' a dream !

END OF THE AULD DOMINIE.*

—:—

IN his last winter, his health, never at any time very "grand," began to decline visibly, and in December the tragic catastrophe occurred as described in the poem which follows :—

'TWAS IN THE DEID O' WINTER.

Wat, wat an' cauld, an' desolate—
Oh ! dreich was that December day,
And wild an' dern, the burns, in full spate,
Rush'd an' roar'd 'tween scaur an' brae.
Owre the droukit, dreepin' yird aye
Clung a dun cloud-murky screen,
That frae mankind, beast, an' birdie,
Hid complete the lift's blue sheen ;
And the gusty winds on hie
Wail'd an' whistled pensivelie
Owre a' the sorry scene.

---

* The unique personage whose strange and dreadful departure at last from this cellar of the universe, in which he had so long burrowed and squacked, was, as is plainly said in the rhyme, assuredly no other than the renowned tenant of the well-known farm of Blaebraes in East Lothian. The deceased was of an unknown age. But he has gone at last, and neither he nor his eccentric performances shall trouble East Lothian or other parts again. Amen. The poor man, we learn, had for a few days prior to his lamentable and dramatic exit been exhibiting, both in public and private life, unmistakable symptoms of extra mental derangement, and developing an outrageous suicidal mania. So much, indeed, was this the case that Nanny, his celebrated and vigorous spouse, had actually to resort to physical force and tie him to his bed, in order to restrain his unconscionable propensities. Unfortunately, during a temporary absence of Mrs Pintail from his bedroom, the patient reached over, and secured a large, sharp table-knife which happened to be lying at the time on a chair

At our onstead, lorn an' lonely,
   Man an' beast were hush'd an' housed ;
Not a cratur' out—deuks only,
   Quacking in the dubs caroused ;
Drowsy dozed the naigs in stable,
   Resting limbs an' cogitating ;
In the courts the nowt did wauble
   To the shed-mouths, ruminating ;
      Cocks an' hens, and poultry fry,
      Cower'd an twitter'd, glum but dry,
   In within their netting.

In the barn the men were packit,
   " Mendin' secks "—nae ploos that day—
Snug an' bien they shoo'd and crackit,
   Tete-á-tete—as guid's a " play."
A' the news the country offer'd
   Crinch for crinch they trockit thrang,
Mulls an' pipes they plied and proffer'd,
   An' merrie jokes an' bars o' sang
      But hoo sune the gloamin' comes !
      " Men, lay by your shears an' thrumbs,
   And hame, lads, let us gang."

near his bedside. With this powerful weapon he appears to have soon
made rope-ends of the heavy coil of hemp with which he was bound to the
bed-posts, for on the return of Agnes in a few minutes to the apartment
she discovered to her terrible dismay that the poor prisoner-patient had
only too surely effected his liberty—with what horrible result the reader
knows. Far and near by thousands this shocking calamity will be read
and deplored, and that notwithstanding the vast age of the poor victim.
In future we may properly tackle to an analysis of the character and
psychological peculiarities which so distinguished " T. P.," but at present
we earnestly beg of all our readers to excuse us. The shock and stun of
the unheard of catastrophe has been too damaging to our system and is
yet much too recent to permit us to contemplate such a labour of love.
Meantime Mrs Pintail may comfort herself for her irreparable loss with
the heartfelt sympathies and condolences of the entire people of the land,
from Maidenkirk to John o' Groat's, for they are, or shall be, hers
indisputably.

Outside, the storm o' rain had given
    Place to ane o' foggy haur—
As if the cluds had a' frae heaven
    Closer drawn to urge the war.
Sair befoul'd an' ill seem'd Nature,
    Ev'n's her latest breath she'd draw,
Thro' the welkin' wing'd nae creature—
    But ae solitary craw,
        Flappin' rookwards, heavilie,
        Just 's thro' Chaos Nick did flie
    When bent on Adam's fa'.

Hamewards trudged the sturdy ploomen
    Thro' the gutters an' the glaur,
When a' at ance a strange—a new man—
    Strode beside them in the haur.
A lang, lank Shape—an' wan Its face was
    As a weirdly daylicht mune,
Whan in Autumn morn the leaf fa's
    Wavering frae its bough abune.
        Silently It stude an' waved them,
        Solemnly by signs It craved them,
    It to follow sune.

'Mang the braes whare Peffer windeth
    There's an ancient Quarry Hole,
Whare in spates the waste flood findeth
    A capacious gruesome goal.
Thereto 'twas the Bogle sped them,
    Thro' the whins wi' ghaistly grace ;
To the very brink It led them,
    Such a spell was in that Face.
        On It fled, an' naething stoppit
        Till—sudden—owre the marge It ploppit
    Deep in the Hole's embrace.

Round they wheel'd and never waited,
   Fear ga'e wings to ilka fit ;
But, as sune's the storm abated,
   Back they cam' an' dragg'd the pit ;
Lo ! they fund a corpse, whase face was
   Faded as a daylicht mune,
Whan in Autumn time the leaf fa's,
   Flickerin', frae the trees abune.
      Whase was it ?　They didna fail
      To see 'twas that o' auld ' Pintail,"
   Kenn'd a' that country roun' !

THE NEW "REAPERS."

[SOME SORROWFUL HARVEST COGITATIONS BY PHARLE

O'RAFFERTY.]

---:---

THIM days no more with huks at all
 Our boys the corn he's switchin',
Such luck agin no more will fall,
 Than ould St Pathrick's preachin'.
All bansthering we now must be—
 We boys—both "rags" and "clever,"
A "stint" to you, a "stint" to me,
 Thin—farewell huk for ever!

Oh! me own heart was bould an' big,
 Whin off I tripped with dearie,
With hip an' elbow, lithe an' trig,
 As e'er left Tipperary!
Kathleen! she know'd me for a man,
 And sure myself did hear her
Say, to the Loudon masther man,
 I was his purtiest shearer.

Me arm it was link't in the whate,
 Loike darlint when I kissed her;
Bad luck, she's dead; she's gone complate,
 Dear Vargin—how I've missed her!
No more Kathleen, nor huk, nor home;
 To these machanes a stranger;

All heedless, loverless, I roam—
A fearful Oirish ranger !

'Tis childer's all they want, ye see,
   To twist and lay the bands—so ;
With two-three boys loike you an' me,
   To make the stuks to stand—so !
The scub machane cooms on loike death,
   Which no man can restrict it,
And shaves, loike min, fall o'er it's path,
   Most devilish unexpicted !

Ould Sathan bred the Scub that made
   This noisy baste, I'm thinkin' ;
Och ! how it's cursed the good ould trade,
   The harvest foon an' drinkin' !
A port !* It's me own sorry eyes
   That's seen more than the talk ow't ;
Thin, a pound a week, sure, were no prize
   To brats 'that scarce could crack ow't !

A boy thin could rest his hand,
   Nor grave nor masther bother,
And joke with lassies in the band
   For swate half hours together.
Thim wos the days ! O swate Kathleen,
   Who's gone to Heaven before me ;
How tinder to this breast you'd lean,
   An' smackin' kisses shower me !

Two horses to a barry chained !
   It licks me noight an' mornin'

---

* A market where harvest wages were fixed for the week. Generally
held on the Monday mornings.

How such a brut by Sathan framed
  Does slick the rushy corn in !
Pat Dolan says, says he, " It is—
  'Tis all the noise as does it,"
And sure, when comin' back it be's,
  The divil a whaysper has it.

It stud, wan day, at breakfast toime,
  Whin we wor busy restin',
The wicked thought coomes in my mind—
  The brut I'd go a-testin'.
The grave was fixin' up her things,
  And many a rap did bring her ;
I felt her teeth—whin, whirr, she sings,
  And halves my purty finger.

My blud be on her iron bones,
  The nasty varmint creatur' ;
May all her teeth be broke with stones,
  And endless chokes await her.
Oh, Kathleen, jewel, up Heaven there,
  Look down on your dear Pharlint,
And bid the angels bless me, dear,
  For oulden times me darlint !

THE AULD FARMER'S LAMENT FOR A WET HARVEST.

—:—

OCH ! sich a dismal harvest day !
  Out thro' the stooks the dreepin' rain
Seeps, seepin'— rottin' corn an' strae,
  An' blastin' a' our hopes again !
The haill wide lift I seek in vain—
  Still thicker grows the cloud array !
How sad noo seems our Loudon plain,
  Whilk erstwhile look'd sae rich an' gay !

Wae sucks, that wearie Eastlin blast,
  Frae yont Dunbar that stormest stoure !
A' ither airts—south, north, or wast—
  At hantrin times grow dull an' dour ;
But thou ! Gude kens nae " simmer shoo'r,"
  Thou brings us whan thou'rt ance owrecast,
But ae lang half-week's constant poo'r
  We maun dree ere thy drunt be past !

O, sirs ! is this the end o' a'
  O' our lang twalmonth's toil an' care ?
To sit thus, feckless, sigh an' blaw,
  Like snools, mere fraits an' vain despair ?
Alack ! I look around me—there,
  In that black east there's prospeck sma'
O' getherin' what aince promis'd fair—
  The richest hairst ere Scotland saw !

Ochone ! gif my dreid fears come true—
  Gif baith the corn and tatties rot—
Syne, what the warld could stap us noo
  Gaun, ae bite, doon disaster's throat !
A mairacle could save us not !
  The dyvor's court we bud gae throo' !
O Lord ! ease thou thy wrath a jot—
  Let not thine ain sae laighly boo !

What wi' rack-rents an' bills to meet—
  Labour a ransom—seasons bad—
The markets farcies—finest wheat
  (Whare it is saved an' can be had)
Selling only sae that ane is glad
  To tak' whatever ane can geet :
A' this—an' mair—mak's me sae mad
  That I, for dounricht teen, could greet !

Oh ! hard art thou—thou wearie warld !
  An' sair, sair are we ding'd by thee !
Frae the blue hichts o' Hope we're hurled,
  Aft in the twinklin' o' an e'e !
Syne whare we crouch in miserie,
  Despair's black banner flaffs unfurled,
And Ruin's sword is threat'ninglie
  Close owre oor heids by factor's swirl'd !

"ANE AULD-FARRANT RAME."

—:—

" QUHAN buddis grene maid faire ye scene
        In oor countrie,
And birddis sange and flowris sprange
        In wud and le ;
Ffor I wald rom, I fersuke hom,
        Maist pensivlie,
And through Loudone—ane hapie lande—
        I wandert fre.

" My doleful mone, like wind, wes gone
        Quhan anes I saw
That hapie lande, with feeldis grande,
        And streme and schaw !
Quhiles, white and bra', ilk fermir's Ha'
        Did pleesandlie
Ye planc ourluke, lik ane Bas Rok
        Ye grait blue Se !

" ' O, hapie land !   O, hapie lande ! '
        Sang in thir gle
Ye merles aroon', ye larks aboon—
        Fra lift and tre !
Quhilk es I heerd, my craig I cleer'd,
        Rapturouslie,
And ' hapie land ! twise hapie land !'
        Maid ansir fre !

" Quhairat ane man upstertit than
            Fra's hedge-side seit—
Ane puir auld man, ane queer auld man,
            Quhom I did greit :
' O, deer auld man ! O, queer auld man !
            Prove thow my fere !—
Expound til me thiss fine countrie,
            This Aiden here !'

" ' Herk ye !' quoth hee, es doon satt wee
            Ane banke upo',
' Thiss fine countrie is al,' says hee,
            ' Ane land of Wo !
Thae ferms thair, ye wene sae faire,
            Ye lairds beelang :
Wee ferminge fok, like al live stok,
            But cum and gang !

" ' With grait payments and rackit rents
            Dett-droon'd are wee ;
, And chokt with wheate and teuch *deid meit*
            Fra owre the se !
Yon Merkit Ha's lang gless ruif braw
            On quhilk sol strones,
Iss broken all in lozens smawl
            With fermirs' grones !

" ' Likwyse thae fock thit mang ous trock
            Hoodwink us sair !
And taxmen crues, and chushie dooze
            Dou pike us bare !
O, giff som cheeld, in thee law skeel'd,
            Wald but deevise
Som akts or bills till stap thaise ills,
            Sans ' Kompromize !'

" ' Wee daurna plow, nir reap, nir soe,
        Bit leeve o' *lease*—
Ane daft fule skreed thit's been ye deid
        Of awl oure race.
Shoo ! *fine countrie !*   Behald,' cried hee,
        Pointing beelo,
' The laust refuse of humbugs huge—
        The Land o' Wo ! '

" Thus havinge skreetch'd, like ane bewitch'd
        Thiss queer auld man
Ran doun ye hill with richt gude will ;
        Yea, roringe, ran !
Quhairat, amaz'd, mysel' I raised
        ('Til kloze ma rame),
And, lawffinge as I'd brust ma hawse,
        Cam' hotchin' hame !"

A BONNIE NOOK ON TYNESIDE.

--:—

THERE is a nook on Tyneside,
 A little, bield, bonnie nook,
That aye to me, the warld wide,
 Is dearer than ony nook ;
Around it tangling woodbine,
Green ivy an' eglantine,
Wi' birks, to mak' a bower, twine
 An' be love's ain nook.

That nook on bonny Tyneside,
 That secret nook I ken weel ;
Oh ! never wi' as fond a tide
 Did river round a shore swiel !
Saft murmurings are stirr'd there,
Sweet is the music heard there,
Rare sings the mavis bird there,
 Gloaming's fa' to peal.

Enfauld that nook on Tyneside,
 Bright spirit powers, evermair !
Oh ! ward that nook on Tyneside
 Wi' ne'er-ending love an' care !
Within its shade we parted,
Ere love was sudden thwarted,
By fell death, sae stane-hearted,
 E'en Jean he wadna spare !

THE AULD TOON—MY BIRTHPLACE.

[WRITTEN IN SICKNESS, ON LAKE HURON, NORTH AMERICA.]

—:—

I RAN aboot the auld toun,
 Fu' happy ran I, years agone,
Sae weal aye fa' the auld toun,
 An' ne'er ae ill licht doun thereon !
There merrilie, by green Tyneside,
 My youthfu' time wing'd fleet awa',—
I was a loon, whase dearest pride
 Was aye the "gamest" deed to shaw ;
And of a valiant laddie-band,
 I chosen was the King to be ;
And he wha daur'd my sway withstand,
 I wat rued his temeritie !

My blessing on that auld toun—
 May never sorrow there be known !
For in an' round that auld toun
 My dearest dwalt this warld upon !
We were a couthie household bien—
 Titties an' billies—sma' an' grown ;
But time our roost has harried clean,
 An' far an' wide the flock is strown !
And Death, fell hunter ! wi' his bow,
 Has sped some deft-aim'd shafts amang 's—
The mother an' seven bairns lie low,
 Like pair birds drapt frae falcon's fangs !

A' round about the auld toun
  Be fairest Nature's mantle thrown !
And pleasant peace that auld toun
  Till Doomsday ever rest upon !
She slumbers by Tyne's hallow'd wave,
  Wha ance could luve rapturouslie ;
She moulders in her early grave
  Wha ance ga'e a' her luve to me !
Oh, Jean, Jean ! by the auld Tyneside
  Nae mair those raptures thrill again !
The simmer comes—but us divide
  Baith hopeless death an' trackless main !

A' bliss enfauld the auld toun,
  And for her kindred sake alone,
Bright spirits ! ward that auld toun,
  An' never clud lat licht upon !
My stricken lassie ! earth looks bleak,
  An' life wi' me is hard to dree ;
My hungry heart 'twere better break,
  Than thole its knawing—craving thee.
Oh, peerless Jean ! what devilish close
  Is this for yon bright life we drew !
Thou in the thief grave must repose,
  I—drift like dust life's desert through !

ON MR ROBERT SHARP, HOTEL PROPRIETOR, LEAVING LINTON.

[READ ON THE OCCASION OF HIS COMPLIMENTARY SUPPER,
7TH DECEMBER 1888.]

—:—

WHAT dreidfu' news is this I hear ?
    Is Robin that we lo'e sae dear—
Is Robin Sharp, wha has nae peer
        For quenching drouth,
Gaun aff to leave us, clean and sheer,
        In waefu' truth ?

For thirty years to our wee toun
He's been, I trow, nae little boon ;
A' our sad cares did Robin droon,
        Day after day,—
Wi' " nips," or caups of foaming broun,
        Rare barley broo !

Of a' your nappies, cheap or dear,
Frae champagne doun to tip'ny beer,
Nae saps ava like his could cheer,
        And warm our heart !—
Our every mortal care and fear
        They gart depart !

On market nichts when we drew nigh
The railway brig, forfocht an' dry,

We'd say, "in Robin's by-and-bye,
　　We'll ease oursel's,"
Syne hoo our mouths wad watter—my !
　　Like muirland wells !

On cattle market days, his house
Was like some great lord duke's lat louse,
The southern dealers, yamp an' crouse,
　　Wad stech an' denner,
As in the days o' auld King Bruce—
　　To Scotland's scunner !

The serving lasses raced an' ran,
Upstairs an' doun, to haud them gaun ;
They daur'dna for ae moment stan'
　　Their breath to draw ;
If ane pat aff—faith, Robin than
　　Shored her the law !

On Hansel Monday afternoons,
Lord—lord, to see the country loons ;
They swarmed like bees owre a' his bouns,
　　And at his board,
His yill an' wheich—they swallowed tuns,
　　An' sang an' roar'd !

But noo, waes me ! he shies awa,
Nae mair for us our nips he'll draw ;
The auld hotel, sae trig an' braw,
　　He'll tend nae mair ;
Below Auld Reekie's castle wa'
　　He seeks his lair.

Weel, weel ; he was a sonsy lad,
Gash, fair an' fat—ne'er sour nor sad,
But smiling aye—richt fain an' glad
  A freend to greet
And shake his hand, and joke like mad,
  And stand a " treat."

Noo he has won his meet reward,
May he for mony a year be spared
To weet his mou' and wag his beard,
  An' tune life's harp ;
Weel on thee is this supper wair'd,
  Douce Robin Sharp.

BY MY NATIVE STREAM.

BY NIGHT.

LO ! by the auld grey castle wa's
    Art wending on,
Where the martin flits as the e'ening fa's,
    As in years bygone ?
Soft an' low, fleet an' flow,
        Awa', awa'.

The stars licht up, as in a dream,
    Auld castled Hailes ;
And o'er thy tide my native stream,
    The owl still wails,
Weird an' shrill, abune the mill—
        " Tu-whoo, tu-whoo ! "

And the ouzel, the craik, and the sedge-singer
    Sing echo forth ;
As the " witching hour," griping night's finger,
    Stalks through the north.
Wi' wan star een, an' wild sick mien—
        Ghaistly, ghaistly.

Ower the auld " strength," like a risen wight,
    A solitary daw
Darkles a moment in the starlight,
    An' flits awa' —
Laughs drear an' clear, the auld mill weir,
        " Awa', awa'."

The same as thou didst ever be,
  My native stream ;
The same—yet ; oh, the same to me
  Thou canst but " seem ; "
  To the world's breast the auld snake 's prest—
    Evil an' care.

BY DAY.

The wagtail an' lone heron ward
  Thy lonely ways !
An' the cushat croods her fond regard
  To the dreaming braes ;
  When the gloaming broods owre the misty woods—
    Wailing, wailing.

Sunlight an' shadow guard thee,
  Like the waited bride ;
An' the brown spate makes thee grand to see—
  Roll on in pride ;
  But gane, dear stream, the grand boy dream—
    Awa', awa' !

LEAVING EAST LINTON.

[WRITTEN FOR AN ORPHAN LASSIE.]

—:—

THE sun shines owre yon grassy lea,
  Whence singing laverocks m'unt the sky ;
An' flocks an' herds sae peacefulie,
  Move here an' there, or wearied lie ;
A' Linton glitters in the glare,
  An' gladsome blink o' bonnie May ;
And licht o' heart is ilk ane there—
  Tho' I maun leave't this Term Day.

And I will never see it mair,
  Oh, never mair again, again !
O wearie me, my heart is sair,
  To say fareweel to a' I ken !
The auld kirkyaird, the water side,
  The jumping trouts, the siller saughs ;
The rocky Linn an's gushing tide,
  Tyne's banks an' braes, an' bonnie haughs !

I daunder dowie thro' the street,
  I stoiter weary up and doun ;
A tether's wound about my heart—
  Its ither end is round this toun.
Oh, bitter fate, that I should dree
  My last day here in maiden prime,
And forsake a' that's dear to me,
  Or e'er will be this side o' time.

Yestreen I wandert to the Law,
  I clamb again the waly brae ;
I kenn'd it was the last o' a'
  The times that I that clim' wad hae.
An' wasna my een wat to see,
  An' wasna my heart wae to feel,
How bonnie is oor auld countrie,
  An' how I loe it a' sae weel.

I've gane to a'where round about—
  To auld Hailes Castle grat fareweel ;
Wi' breaking heart an' lingering foot,
  Pressmennan left and bonnie Biel.
An' Binnin' Wood where aft I stray'd
  Wi' Jamie in the dear langsyne ;
The Auld Wa's, Round Taps, an' Langside,
  Pencraig, an' up an' doun a' Tyne !

And noo, this warld hauds nocht to me
  But the sad memorie o' them a',
O Linton ! what wey should it be
  That I frae thee maun shog awa' ?
Here, in thy dear lap, wad I rest,
  Here, in thy bosie, live an' dee—
My native nook, my native nest—
  But Fate says, "Na! it canna be !"

FAREWEEL!

[WRITTEN FOR A FRIEND LEAVING HAILES COTTAGE.]

—:—

WHITE, white lies the winter roun' the auld castle
wa',
An' ruin'd keep an' toorie are wreath'd wi' the snaw,
As time draws near to lea' them, tho' but deid wa's they
be,
Amid the snaws o' winter they dearer grow to me !

For they mind me o' langsyne, when in the dear old days
I ran a thochtless lassie o'er Tyne's sweet banks an' braes,
An' roun' an' roun' the Castle, like bairn roun's mither's
knee,
I grew up, little dreaming how dear it was to me !

Here I a maid was courted—was wooed an' wed an' a',
Here a' the bairns were born, an' ane was ta'en awa',
Here we've been lang sae happy—the bairns, gudeman, an'
me —
It hurts like death to think o' this parting that maun be !

Never again, O never to ca' this house our hame !
Never again, O never this auld fireside to claim !
Thro' a' the lang years coming the strangers' place 'twill be,
When we are gane for ever—the bairns, gudeman, an' me !

The bairns they cling to "mither," the gudeman downa
    speak,
I cheery-like tend to them when my heart's like to break ;
An' frae this ben-room window, when nae ane's bye to see,
What longing looks I'm taking o' the auld countrie !

Ah ! wae is me, thou robin that singest at the door,
Ae waefu' lilt o' sorrow is a' thy birdie's store,
A wail for byegane simmer that soon returns to thee ;
But our bonnie auld hame—never, can time gi'e back to
    me !

To say " Fareweel for ever," ye bonnie banks an' braes,
An' fare ye weel, Tyne river, that I lo'ed a' my days ;
Farcweel Traprain and Kippie ! fareweel the dear auld
    Mill,
The brig across the water, the fit-road up the hill !

But we a' maun say "fareweel "—on earth we canna stay ;
" Fareweel !" "fareweel !" "farcweel !"—day crieth unto
    day ;
The warld is wide an' wearie, an' hard is life, I trew—
A touch, a turn of fortune—the *auld* is changed to *new !*

But oh ! my heart is dowie, sae weel it lo'ed this nest,
An' a' its ties asunder this flicht to rive at last !
But take this flicht I *maun*, nor spurn at Fate's decree,
An' gae seek anither hame in a strange countrie !

o

AULD CASTLED HAILES.

[ON LEAVING FOR A FOREIGN LAND.]

—: —

MEANDER on an' glide awa',
   My gentle Tyne ;
Wend by Hailes' ruined castle wa'
   Like stream divine !
Too soon to me shalt thou hidden be,
   For aye, for aye.

" For ever ! " oh, the heart is sair—
   For ever, ever !
And I shall scan thee with proud eye nae mair,
   Never ! oh, never !
Wail, thou wintry gales, through castled Hailes—
   Och hone the day !

Here my young footsteps lov'd thy keep,
   Romantic Hailes !
What time the howlet, weird an' deep,
   The moon assails.
And here—oh, here—I trysted here,
   My Jean, sweet Jean !

Here the martin and the water ouzel,
   When gloamings wane,
Shall come, sweet summer, musical,
   When I am gane ;
And the cushet crood in the drowsy wood,
   Like Nature's saul !

The jenny wren an' the sedge singer,
  The wagtail, sae spree ;
In the golden e'enings here shall linger,
  While unremembered Me
Drees wind and lee in a far countrie—
  Alas ! alas !

O drift my bark where earth 's Lethé—
  Ye westlin' gales—
Holds memories of thee far owre the sea,
  Auld Castled Hailes !
Fareweel this day, fareweel for aye—
  Fareweel ! fareweel !

JEANIE'S FAREWEEL.

— :—

FAREWEEL, thou bonnie Auld Hailes,.
  An' a' thy broomy knowes sae fair ;
I'm broken doun in misery,
  To say—" Fareweel for evermair."
Oh, had this warld a warld been,
Whare justice aye stood poortith's freen',
This weary day I hadna seen,
  Nor my heart pang'd sae fu' o' care.

Fareweel, thou auld Castle wa's,
  Whare Tyne sae fondly lingers bye,
In 's bosom proudly cherishing
  Thy hoary shadows, braid an' high.
As in the stream sae faithfully
Thy ruins deep below we see,
Sae true thy cherished memory
  In my leal hear shall ever lie !

Fareweel thou blooming hawthorn,
  Whare my dear laddie trysted me,
When blackbirds sweetly chirrupit
  To greet the e'ening star on hie !
Nae mair, thou blooming thorn, nae mair
Will I to thy sweet shade repair,
To meet my gentle laddie there—
  But wander to a far countrie.

'Sae fareweel, bonnie Auld Hailes,
  An' a' thy broomy knowes sae fair,
An' saugh an' hawthorn blossoming—
  Fareweel, fareweel, for evermair !
The little birds on restive wing
Tak' up the strain an' seem to sing,
" Oor Jeanie's gaun awa', puir thing—
  Fareweel, fareweel, for evermair !"

A SUNDAY IN MAY.

—:—

I.—AT PRESTONKIRK CHURCH : MORNING.

BY the river, flowing sweetly,
  In the time, when, bright and featly,
Young May cam' to braird the corn,
And it upward sprung to greet her,
Gleaming green, and fresher—sweeter,
  In the dew o' early morn !

Doun the gate I quietly daunder'd
To the Kirk, and sadly ponder'd
  On the lives o' rich and puir ;
The peer and peasant in their hames,
The pomp and poverty that shames
  Alike their joy and care.

When, lo, the Kirk ! sae heichly cantled
On its knowe, and ivy mantled,
  'Mang the tombs fu' sacredlie !
Large an' hamely 'tis—nae feature
Grand or gorgeous, nor in stature
  As our " Lamps " o' Lothian be.

But if here Man's work be barren,
Fairest Nature doth adorn
  Sweet an' rare the hallow'd scene !
Wood and water, corn fields fertile—
Teeming with luxuriance—kyrtle .
  This God's Acre like a queen.

Now the worshippers draw hither ;
Men and women, a' thegither,
   Fill the House o' God within.
Hark ! their Sang o' Praise they're singing,
From frail sinful hearts 'tis winging
   To the God who hateth sin.

Next the shepherd, young and fervent,
A true leader and Christ's servant,—
   For this great flock rev'rently,
With no mock ecclesiastic,
But, with heart-born words, makes plastic
   Their souls' wants to soar on high.

Then the Inspired Word he readeth,
Earnestly, as when he pleadeth
   At the Divine Cross for man :
All about the auld devices—
Offerings and sacrifices—
   " Needful in Jehovah's plan."

Anon the sermon.   (Whare the text was,
If in Psalms or Eccles'astes—
   Haith ! I really have forgot !
Surely, surely 'twas from David—
But as I its gist have savèd,
   Book and chapter matter not.)

From the simple words—" Then let us
Into the Lord's House beget us,"
   Such a theme's developèd
Of fresh thought and reasoning subtle—
Yet true Gospel ring and metal—
   Knox seems risen from the dead.

Logic, eloquence—ay, passion—
But devoid the clap-trap fashion
    That obtains with narrow minds ;
Sensible—and credit craving
Only for what's worth believing—
    Ev'ry word a heart-home finds.

Leeze me on such halesome preachers ;
Best exemplars—helpers—teachers,
    Leaders fraught with God-like powers,
On the Master—all reliance ;
Hand in hand with sense and science—
    May such priests be ever ours !

II.—AT HOME : MIDNIGHT.

The fire burns dimly in the grate,
    The lamp upon the table—so,
As I sit questioning my fate,
    Neither in joy nor in woe ;
I know that I must surely die,
    But what death is I cannot tell ;
No surety unto me draws nigh
    Beyond the dead man's fun'ral bell.
But I have hope, and hope means life,
    For all the tongues of Nature say
That naught is useless—so this strife
    A calm Hereafter may repay :
If that hope's false, this Universe,
    To all mankind, is but a curse.

WRITTEN ON A BEAUTIFUL OCTOBER DAY.

—:—

HOW mystic, mild, an' meek seems this wondrous
harvest time,
When life an' death do meet at the turning o' the clime ;
An' between them, lyart-mantled, wi' her patient mien an'
sweet,
Autumn comes to throw her off'ring at their never-resting
feet.

Fruitful matron !—heir an' parent o' the wondrous annual
round,
In thy calm an' grey-eyed visage beameth wisdom forth
profound ;
In thy ruddy placid visage true beneficence is seen,
Care an' love for every creature—open-handed, god-like
queen !

'Twixt the yokes o' anxious labour either side entangling
me,
In an awe o' gratitude do I pause an' gaze on thee ;
In the thicket o' my toils this meal-hour is as a loan,
Or an open in a forest, thro' which spacious Heaven is
shown.

Thou wi' fading leaves art buskit—but the berries cluster
red,
Whare the mellow licht encircles, like a crimson band, thy
head.

In the purple hazy distance streams thy wonder-woven
    robe—
Countless shades o' green and russet to the gleaming azure
    throb.

But, fareweel, for ev'n thou fleetest, gorgeous queen and
    bountiful ;
Soon thy throne another filleth of a sterner law and rule ;
Even now I hear him rousing as thy flashing glories wane ;
May thy garner all suffice us, till thou heapest it again !

"MITHER CALEDON."

[WRITTEN IN MY BOYHOOD.]

——:——

SHED that veil o' cloud atwain,
 Loot owre me wi' smile sae fain,
Listen to thy callant's strain —
  Mither Caledon !

Roll on the ages owre thee !
Wallace eras nae mair be ;
But thou—right and liberty !
  Mither Caledon !

Generations, law an' line,
Tumble frae that lap o' thine ;
Thou ! stern an' rude, but heart divine—
  Mither Caledon !

High in thine eternal seat,
Eagle-eyed the epochs greet ;
Glean their fair flowers at thy feet--
  Mither Caledon !

Arise ! and take the " vaward,"
Girt with righteous purpose hard—
Thine old shield and surest guard,
  Mither Caledon !

Ahead ! scan out the march-way,
Point a warld to light an' day,
High on hill-tops, and away—
    Deathless Caledon !

WILLIAM WALLACE.

[WRITTEN IN BOYHOOD.]

—:—

THEY slew thee—did they ?   Let it be !
   No more : it cannot be undone,
   But, truly, could thy fate back run,
I would not wish one breath for thee.

The tyrant and the hero sleep—
   Lift up thy heavens, God, on high,
   Let light abound, let darkness die,
Let truth thy utmost confines keep.

The tyrant and the hero, then,
   In equal, perfect justice show—
   The fiendish lust—against the glow
Of truest, noblest love for men.

He, high beyond all factions, grew,
   And, despite them, his purpose held,
   Through petty turmoil, still unquell'd
The hero rose—we see him now.

All power, the worldling's power and gold,
   To stoop and take were at his feet ;
   Or, earthly death, defamed to greet,
And let sure time his worth unfold.

And, all undoubting, death was ta'en,
　Through torture on the traitor's tree !
　O Wallace ! never liberty,
For this forsakes our land again !

THE BATTLE OF BANNOCKBURN.

[WRITTEN IN MY BOYHOOD.]

—-:—

FAST phalanx'd on Bannock side—
 Oh ! look a risen land ;
For one last stroke for freedom dear,
 Take up her final stand !
  Confess'd in heaven's fixed decree—
  'Tis life, 'tis death—but liberty !

Her pennons, dyed in war's red tide,
 And banners shaped in fight,
Flap memories about the winds,
 And wrongs of Wallace wight !
  A thousand arms shall pledge the foe—
  A thousand fold the tyrant's blow

De Boune and Clifford, heralding,
 The dawn of freedom's morn,
First cross the weirds in deadly strife,
 The foes of Bannockburn.
  And summer Sol bursts out to see,
  A sacrifice to liberty !

A voice, as of a mighty wind
 Up from a redeem'd sea,
Sweeps every wrong and woe away
 With one word—Victory !
  And smiling peace, so long forlorn,
  Hallows the field of Bannockburn !

JOHN KNOX.

—:—

LIKE lion-fronted isle sublime
   That sheer from ocean seek'st the sky—
Above the levelled waste of Time
   Thou towerest heavenward, huge, and high
     Between this light and yon dark past,
     An adamantine barrier cast !

And as such isle, sun-rising east
   Hangs in his orient o'er the sea,
Art thou, o'er all time set amidst,
   The gratitude of all the free
     Thou, stable midst unstable, stood
     The worthiest for thy country's good.

For thou with fix'd soul didst pursue
   Thy purpose sacred—light for man,
Nor fear nor mortal weakness drew
   Thee from the goal one wayward span,
     But bursting the chaotic night,
     Thy one aim cleft—" Let there be light !'"

And there was light ! and evermore,
   Sphered radiant in that light, art thou !—
A glowing orb amid the gloir
   That star-wreathes Fame's eternal brow,
     And tints with amaranthine ray
     Time's passing turbid flood for aye !

JULIE-ANNIE.

NATURE, robed in snowy white,
As she is this cold March night,   .
Draws again my thoughts to bright
                    Julie-annie !

Fair, in Fancy's waking eye,
Lo ! the maiden passes by,
First of maidens, I descry
                    Julie-annie !

In my sad heart's inmost core,
She's enshrinèd as of yore,
Where she reigneth evermore—
                    Julie-annie !

From her queen-like, ample brow,
Jetty locks the breezes blow,
Screening Grecian bust of snow—
                    Julie-annie !

Bright, beneath each fringèd lid,
Dewy orbs swim in their pride,
Beaming love on every side,
                    Julie-annie !

Cheeks, whose lustre mocks the morn,
They thy youth and heart adorn,
For thereon that heart is worn,
                    Julie-annie !

P

Soft rose lips, where sweetness piles
Sweetest bliss in sweetest smiles,
And young Love triumphs in his wiles,
    Julie-annie !

Thus, and thus before me now
In this night of moonlit snow,
Flits thy virgin vision so,
     Julie-annie !

Sages say all worlds have spun
Ever round a centre sun,
So my fate round thee does run,
     Julie-annie !

But thy bright orb's sphere is o'er
In this dark world evermore,
Long, long time it set before,
     Julie-annie !

THE FA' O' THE LEAF.

[A FRAGMENT.]

—:—

WINTER trips on autumn's heels
    To her ither climes awa' ;
Dark grow the woods an' gray the fiel's
    Where the fitfu' sunbeams fa' ;
Gloaming comes wi' afternoon,
    Hastening nicht to hide the grief ;
Luna, pale, amid the gloom,
    Mourns her earthy chief ;
Streams rin wildly to the sea,
Winds sing weirdly through the tree—
    At fa' o' the leaf !

Summer's requiem—hear it sung
    O'er wide ocean in the night,
When the trumpet storms are strung
    Wild as Neptune's own delight !
Hear the staves upon the shore
    Struck by Boreas in his glee !
Where Tantallon's ruins tower
    Ruin's tale will be,
Misery an' wreck will cry
Nature's dirges to the sky
    Frae the listless sea !

Hear them through the moaning wood,
 Hear them o'er the dreary plain,
Down the valley o' the flood,
 O'er the waters o' the main !
Read them in the murky sky
 In the hour o' closing day,
In the dowie flowers that lie
 Drooping by the way !
List them in the robin's lore
Lilted at your cottage door
 A' the cheerless day !

What eerie winds are sweeping
 Over Nature's bier !
Winter's arms are creeping
 Round the dying year !
And a never-fairing shower
 Comes flickering on the blast —
Dead summer's worn dower,
 With which sweet May her dress'd ;
And o'er his naked feet
 The leaves young winter strews,
And binds with wind and weet
 The vestment round his thews.

EAST LOTHIAN.

—:—

A THREE-FOLD picture—moorland, plain, and sea—
Behold our Lothian, limn'd so matchlessly !
Her rocky isles and castellated shore—
The blue waves fondling them for evermore ;
The white-wing'd ships, her sea-world couriers given,
Circling around her like the birds of heaven ;
Her heathy moors, a waving background grand—
Dark forests rolling to her happy strand !
Soft-contour'd hills upspringing from her breast,
Where Labour struggles and is lull'd to rest ;
Crystalline streams sweet-babbling thro' her vales,
Like wandering maidens singing true love tales !—
Her fields, her plains, and, smoking far and near,
Her freemen's peasant homes—to Peace and Virtue dear !

AULD LANGSYNE.

—:—

WHEN gloomy dool lies heavy on the heart,
    An' darkens a' the warld to our e'e,
How fondly backward do our fancies start
An' revel in the realms o' memory !
The golden days o' yore we live again—
We trace sweet childhood's paths and flowery plain—
We rin ance mair the raids our boyhood ran—
We haunt the haunts o' our romantic youth
(That yett o' Eden, whaur real life began,
An' we war' thrust furth on this world uncouth !)—
We linger in the scenes, lang years forlorn,
Whaur early manhood strode, an' love was born,
An' still the mair is loved the mair we tine
That glamourie buskit time—dear, hallow'd, Auld Langsyne !

SELECTED SONGS.

THE KNOX MEMORIAL.

[SONG WRITTEN FOR, AND SUNG AT, THE PUBLIC CONCERT
HELD IN AID OF THE FUNDS OF THE INSTITUTION.]

—:—

YE wha reck our Scottish name
    Fit wi' the warld's first to ally,
Match wi' thy gift this cherish'd fame,
    An' round our Knox Memorial rally.
Our kindly plans, as Scotland scans,
    Auld memories crowd thick upon her ;
Wi' gleamin' e'e, her children free—
    She points out Knox for foremost honour.

There Resby, Craw, an' Hamilton,
    An' seer-like Wishart—daunted never !—
Were in her glorious cause struck down,
    An' wear their martyr crowns for ever.
But he wha came wi' noblest aim
    An' crowned their wark wi' highest glory,
Hath not a stane, for a' our gain,
    In his loved land to tell his story.

But hark ye, Scots ! it shall not be,—
    Scotland's leal in heart, tho' boreal,

Tho' maybe late, we'll surely see
    A gratefu' country's Knox Memorial !
That day come soon ! his native toun—
    Her Lamp o' Lothian burnin' brighter,
May woo Tyneside wi' leesome pride,
    An' daur the envious warld to wyte her.

For weel ye trow his " cairn " shall be
    Nae feckless monumental ruckle,
But ae great schule o' learnin'—free
    To whilk our deftest lads may buckle ;
Where ane an' a', baith puir an' braw,
    May pluck the tree o' ample knowledge,
Or at the door, for little store,
    Plume their young wings for highest college.

Then rally, rally round our flag,
    Nae Scot sae dowie he may rally
An' somewhat aid, tho' 's means may lag,
    Will prove him to the world our ally.
Lang life an' power to young Balfour,
    Honour to Scott, an' years to wear it ;
An' eke each name, we proudly claim,
    Posterity will yet revere it.

Then rally, rally ! O ye Scots !
    Oh, what is warld's gear to honour ?
Come wi' your placks, your crowns, your notes,
    Throw aff ingratitude wi' scunner !
Was not John Knox—ye heedless folks—
    The maker o' the weal ye thrive in ?
And can ye now mair wisely show
    Your thanks than aid the scheme we strive in ?

This ancient burgh, Haddington,
Wi' royal charter, rights, an' laws still,
That gave us Scotia's wisest son,
Maun keep the lead in freedom's cause still.
Nae faint turncoat our auld grey Goat,
She'll ever to the age conform her !
Sae now her cry—" Let faction die,
And honoured be our Great Reformer !"

"FAR AWA'."

[WRITTEN BY REQUEST FOR THE GLASGOW HADDINGTONSHIRE
ASSOCIATION, FOR THEIR ANNUAL FESTIVAL.]

—:—

YE banded friends for noble aims,
  Wha kythe the kindly Loudon face !
Compatriots St Mungo names,   ·
  The wale o' Scotia's waly race !
Far wander'd frae the native place
  Atween the sea an' Lammerlaw,—
This nicht in fancy we'll retrace
  The dear calf-ground that's far awa' !

By castled and cathedral'd Tyne
  In gratefu' thought we'll backward stray,
Where Knox immortal sprang lang syne,
  An' rising Balfour hath his sway.
Where erst we sped life's early day,
  An' pu'd the mellow hip and haw,
By mony a shaw an' breezy brae,
  In bonny Loudon far awa'.

Oh, Balfour ! honoured, reverèd name,
  Where'er a Union Scot prevails !
Wi' growing ardour ward thy fame—
  Romantic, Tyne-trothed, castled Hailes !
Around thee cling Queen Mary tales,
  Like ivy round thy ruin'd wa'—

Still greener aye as time assails
   Thy riven ramparts far awa' !

Atween Tantallon on the shore
   An' far lone Soutra on the muir,
To deeds heroic aft of yore
   Our Scotian fathers kindled there ;
And tho' auld Noll did fool us sair
   At Hill o' Doon, through Leslie's flaw,
At Prestonpans we made it square,
   Where, like flay'd sheep, they ran awa'.

Traprain, the Bass, Pressmennan Loch,
   The Garletons an' Gullane hie,
Frae Wallyford to Auldhamstock,
   Landmark our matchless auld countrie !
And, worthy such a land to be,
   The Loudon lads and lassies a'
In fame an' honour tap the tree,
   And lead the race, ev'n far awa'.

The pearl an' pride o' Scottish shires,
   We'll roose auld Loudon till we dee ;
The trusty sons of trusty sires,
   Bright honour shall our device be !
And love fraternal, true an' free,
   Shall closer still an' closer draw—
Despite how rank or place decree—
   The Loudon laddies far awa' !

AITHIE GRAEME.*

--:--

OH ! I'm a rovin', gangrel loon,
    Wi' lichtsome pouch an' hairt !
Frae Berwick Brig to Brig of Doon
    I ply my whistlin' airt.
At ilka weel-kenned clachan toun
    I'm never grudged a hame,
To screen frae scaith, when nicht sets doun,
Or frien's to kett the lyart croon
    O' puir, auld Athie Graeme !

I've cheer'd the ways o' youth an' e'il
    Thae thretty years and mair ;
An' binna when I tint my Nell,
 ˙ I've little pree'd o' care.
That gruesome day !—I mind it weel !—
    In route for Kelso Fair.
She teuk the tout, near Galashiel,
That fairly nickit winsome Nell,
    An' snaw'd my raven hair !

The flow'r was on the rowan tree,
    The blossom on the heath,
Beside a spring, aneath a brae,
    We coor'd to gether breath.

---

* A wandering penny-whistle player, who has now joined the majority.

" Come, Athie, dearie, play," quo' she,
" John Anderson, my jo !
I'm maybe wrang o' what's to be ;
But something, Athie, loors on me—
    That hechts death's comin' blow ! "

She dee'd that vera nicht.   Sin' syne
    I've wandered high an' low,
Still dearer to me, an' divine,
    Grows winsome Nell, my jo !
But mony a tear, for auld lang syne,
    Doth blin' auld Athie's e'e !
This human heart mak's sic a shine !
An' downa eithly memory tine,
    In even a man like me !

THE BROKEN BANK.*

—:—

WAUR than auld times, when deidly weir
   Made Caledon blude sairly,
This last sad fleg is like, I fear,
  To break her auld heart fairly ;
Ane waesome soun's in a' her touns,
  An' hill an' dale, wi' bitter wail,
Tell that the blow has e'en brought low,
  The land that prosper'd rarely !

As on Fa'kirk an' Flodden fiel's
  She lost thro' treason merely,
Sae now she fa's by fause-loon chiels,
  Betrayed—dishonour'd clearly !
Throo a' her bounds, this cry resounds :
  Wae worth their name that wrought such shame,
An' aim'd the blow, that brought sae low,
  The land we lo'e right dearly !

But while thae traitor knaves their meed
  In durance wait securely,
O wha the stricken deer will heed—
  The wreck'd an' ruin'd surely ?

---

* This song was written to be sung at a Public Concert which was to
have been held in aid of the sufferers by the collapse of the City of
Glasgow Bank, but which, however, like its object, "collapsed" too
soon.

Will nae strong hand, owre a' Scotland,
  Be sheuken out, and raze the blot
That wad defame her matchless name,
  An' rieve her honour purely ?

Behin' Fa'kirk cam' Bannockburn !
  We paid back Flodden dearly !
Sae noble plenty may return,
  Whaur poortith pinches sairly !
Let each true Scot, in ha' an' cot,
  Grip hand in hand—a dauntless band ;
Wi' word an' deed, to serve in need,
  The land they lo'e sincerely !

Then wae an' want, a long fareweel,
  An' routhie times come early ;
Fareweel, deil greed ! for aye, fareweel—
  Leal Scotland fits thee puirly !
All hail ! again thou goodly train—
  Stern worth an' truth, an' love an' ruth,
That raised sae high, in days gane by,
  The land we lo'e sae dearly !

THE PLOUGHMAN.

—:—

DRINK a bumper to the ploughman,
  Pledge him in a cup profound,
Toast him as our strong and true-man
  With all honours round and round :
      Here's the brawny, buirdly ploughman !
      Here's the world's breadwinner true !
      Drink a beaker to the ploughman—
      To the dregs drink—Speed the Plough!

Thro' the bitter days of winter,
  Cold and wet he guides the share ;
Toiling on till night present her
  Warm fireside and cottage fare—
      Here's the brawny, &c.

In the wakening spring-time speeding,
  What a priest in power is he !
Striding forth—the broad earth seeding
  That her children filled may be.
      Here's the brawny, &c.

On thro' sweltry scorching summer,
  Never lagging, late and soon ;
Urging Nature heap her garner,
  Like one gracious, princely boon !
      Here's the brawny, &c.

Then he grasps the golden harvest,
　Sweeps the wide fields at a word ;
Till from happy east to far west
　He the world with rowth has stored !
　　Here's the brawny, buirdly ploughman !
　　Pledge him in a cup profound—
　　Toast him as our strong and true-man
　　With all honours—round and round !

LITTLE LAUCHIN' JEAN.*

— :—

THRO' stookit fields o' yellow corn
I held me to my dearie,
But dowie thochts, an' dool forlorn,
Made my heart wae and wearie.
I watna hoo this mood had come—
Maybe 'twas Autumn's sheen ;
But weel I wat wha cleard the gloom—
My little lauchin' Jean !

The genty, merry, lo'esome lass
Was waitin' by the style,
But crooch'd ahint a whinny bus',
To tease me wi' her wile.
Thocht I, " What's up ? nae lassie here ;
She promised, too, yestreen "—
When skirl on skirl brak' on my ear
Frae little lauchin' Jean.

Sour dool forsook me then at ance,
I stood 'maist gyte wi' joy,
An' join'd her mirth—as if by chance—
Proud victim o' her ploy.

---

* The above song has been set to music by Mr G. Henschel, of London,
and the composition has been very favourably received. Copies may be
had from Mr Wm. Sinclair, Haddington, and Messrs Stanley Lucas,
Weber, Pitt & Hartzfeld, Ltd., 84 New Bond Street, London, W. Price,
2s net.

O warld ! what bliss was mine in turn
  That heaven-like harvest e'en,
Amang the stooks o' gowden corn
  Wi' little lauchin' Jean !

Her wee saft loof enclasped my arm,
  Her e'e look'd up in mine ;
We neither trow'd nor minded harm—
  Leal love is pure an' kin'.
An' never mair ae fit o' care
  That nicht daur'd intervene ;
My only smart was wae to part
  Wi' little lauchin' Jean.

" RECIPROCITY."

—:—

HAE ye ne'er heard o' the braw shepherd lad,
   Wha wons 'wa' doun n'ar the sea,
An' has whittled a rung, a' our cares to blaud—
   Ca'd Res-e-pros-e-tee ?
     " Just " Res-e-pros-e-tee,
     " Fair " Res-e-pros-e-tee !
He'll cudgel the croons o' the foreign loons
     Wi' Res-e-pros-e-tee !

This shepherd bold is a discreet lad,
   And ane cunning carle is he !
Sae he has been kuitlin', sin' times grew bad,
   At Res-e-pros-e-tee.
     " Just " Res-e-pros-e-tee, &c.

Gin Jonathan tax a' our kirns an' clouts,
   Why should his wheat come free ?
" Gie him tit for tat," the shepherd he shouts,
   Wi' Res-e-pros-e-tee !
     " Just " Res-e-pros-e-tee,
     " Fair " Res-e-pros-e-tee !
We'll blister the croons o' the foreign loons
     Wi' Res-e-pros-e-tee !

LINTON LYNN.

—:—

WE had a wee pownie—we had but the ane,
    An' when that ane crokit—O, we had nane !
The siller's sae scarce aye an' hard to win—
        Dear Meg, what gar't thou dee ?

We draggit her doon to the banks o' the Tyne,
An' wi' oor gleg gillies we skinn'd her fu' fine ;
And intil the stream we whammel'd her syne,
        A feast for troots to be !

But that e'enin' a dreidfu' rain there set in,
And the river neist day full spate it did rin—
Sae aff soom'd oor pownie to Linton Lynn,
        Aboot the hoor o' three.

" Oh, murder ! a murder—if there ever was ane ! "
The fock they a' cried, when, awantin' the skin,
They saw the auld pownie skyte ower the Lynn ;
        A ghaistly sicht to see.

Syne wi' poles an' muck-hawks they a' then did rin,
The " murdered manic " to grab oot o' the Lynn ;
But nocht but a *pownie wantin' the skin*
        Could thae fule bodies see !

"THE CHARTERIS DYKES."*

[THE AULD DOMINIE'S SANG.]

—:—

WHEN comin' roond about the dykes,
    Daunerin' roond aboot the dykes,
An aingel I foregather'd wi'—
    When comin' roond aboot the dykes !

" Kind sir," she says, " pray tell me true,
    Is this the gate to auld Blaebraes ?"
" Sweet lassie ! I will tell thee true—
    I gang that gate mysel' the day !"
               When comin', &c.

We wandered on—oh, she was fair !
    My heart frae Nanny she withdrew ;
Love revel'd in her gowden hair,
    His palace was her bonnie mou' !
               When comin', &c.

At last we reached the auld Blaebraes ;
    Losh ! Agnes rins to meet my doo—
" Dear sister, welcome hame ! " she says—
    The " aingel " lauch'd till she was blue !

When comin' roond aboot the dykes,
    Daunerin' roond aboot the dykes,
Nae mair yer aingels foist on me—
    When comin' roond aboot the dykes !

---

* The high stone wall bounding the Amisfield policies on the south,
near Haddington.

NOW WILLIE'S AWA.*

—:—

NOW blythe lilt the birds doun the bonnie Tyne valley,
   The larks hover hie o'er the green Kippielaw ;
How sweet 'twere to roam thro' the springtime wi' Willie,
   But how weary to wander, now Willie's awa !
The snaw-hoards on Soutra, the saft win's are thawing,
   The simmer's renew'd to the muirland an' lea ;
The swallows come back an' the blossom is blawing—
   A' nature's restored, but na' Willie to me !

The snawdrap an' vi'let, in nooks bield and shady,
   The primrose an' daisy —the fairest o' a' ;
The hawthorn blooming, the green-spreading meadow,
   Wad wyse me to wander—but Willie's awa !
Ah ! never again, by the green shaw an' meadow,
   While Tyne bickers doun sunny-starr'd to the sea,
Shall I wander at e'ening, an' hear my dear laddie,
   Roose nature sae deeply and dearly to me !

The setting sun beats on the braes o' Phantassie,
   An' cleeds in gold haze the green Kippielaw !
The dew freshens nature, sae green an' sae grassy—
   How blest wad I be werena Willie awa !
O thou mellow mavis, the e'ening enchanting,
   Till th' kindling stars thrill i' the blue lift sae hie !
How sweet was thy sang, in yon gloaming-hushed plantin',
   When in true love we trysted—my Willie an' me !

---

* Written on the occurrence of a melancholy incident in real life.

O hush ye, blythe birds, doun the bonnie Tyne valley,
　　O hush ye, sweet larks, o'er the green Kippielaw !
What recks how ye sing, an' ye sing na back Willie !
　　Your woodnotes are wailings noo Willie's awa !
The snawdrift, o'er Soutra, in tempest was blawing,
　　An' bleak was the scene on the day he did dee !
But bleaker an' darker is sorrow's nicht fa'ing—
　　This mirk nicht o' death—that parts Willie and me !

NORTH BERWICK NELL

—:—

JOY, joy, could I but have her,
　Could I catch this peerless belle ;
Only at death's yett I'd leave her—
　Charming, sweet North Berwick Nell !

The Linton lasses wash an' kame,
　An' ilk ane thinks she 's nae sma' swell ;
But they're a' ghaists awa' frae hame,
　As sune's they meet North Berwick Nell !
　　Joy, joy, &c.

Them at Dunbar, an' Ada's toun*
　Wi' saws an' pents busk up to " tell ; "
But when a's dune, hoo dun an' broun
　They look beside North Berwick Nell !
　　Joy, joy, &c.

Thou'rt in thy fisher graith an' goon,
　Short coaties to thy knees—a belle,
That needna fear to shaw thy shoon,
　Nor thy twa legs, North Berwick Nell !
　　Joy, joy, &c.

What tho' thy minnie flytes an' scalds,
　An' thy auld dad goes on the " gell ; "
Such virtue to thine ainsel' halds,
　Thy freends seem saunts, North Berwick Nell !
　　Joy, joy, &c.

---
　　　　* Haddington.

Upo' her back the wauchty creels,
　She thraws as eithly in a spell
As yon " half-nabs " do their manteels—
　Nae dolly jade's North Berwick Nell !
　　Joy, joy, &c.

Her crabs an' haddies ilka morn,
　Owre a' the toun she tak's to sell ;
Wi' ne'er a fin' does she return ;
　Wha could resist North Berwick Nell ?
　　Joy, joy, &c.

Her face is like the rising sun,
　Whan first it peeps in Lowrie's dell,
Sae roguish red, sae fu' o' fun,
　An' love an' glee 's North Berwick Nell !
　　Joy, joy, &c.

Her form is like the spreading aik's,
　That grows abune St Mungo's Well ;
A queen-like lass that never quakes—
　What storm could wrack North Berwick Nell !
　　Joy, joy, &c.

Ye gods wha shute to man his lot
　As thou think fit—or ill or well—
Keep what thou list, but, oh ! ye gods,
　Grant me, grant me, North Berwick Nell !

　　Joy, joy, could I but have her,
　　　Could I cleek unto this belle ;
　　Only at death's yett I'd leave her—
　　　Gallant, rare, North Berwick Nell !

KYLEY BROUN.

[THE DECEIVING DROVER OF PERTH.]

—:—

A' ye men folk come to buy
   At canny Cupar Fair,
Hielan' cattle, stots, or kye,
   Of your spare brass beware !
There is a little Highlander—
A man of lies and mickle stir
Tak' ye tent—beware o' " her,"
   An' keep an e'e aroun'.
He'll blaw his beasts up to the skies—
Swear ilk ane 's ta'en ta Hielan' prize,
An' toss his heid—this Man o' Lies—
   As 'twerna Kyley Broun.

In his ain shire he flees aboot
   An' buys the auld wives' kye
(Nae doubt he'd steal them, tail an' clout
   If he but daur't to try).
Within his byre, aff coat he flings,
An' binds ilk Crum wi' wicked strings—
Frae ilka horn risps aff the " rings "
   To swear she's young, the loon.
He'll blaw his beasts, &c.

His stirks he wiles frae Hielan' herds
   Wi' tales o' strong Glenlivet,

But when the barrel comes frae Perth,
　An's pree't nae man will have it.
He starves the young, he clips the auld—
Dog-kennel victims gingers bauld,
No matter what—if they're but sald,
　　An' he can clear a croon.
He'll blaw his beasts, &c.

His puir auld mither's heart he'll break,
　If it can break ava
Her auld red head, I trow, alake!
　E'en now is streak'd wi' snaw.
It's weel to wish she mayna see
The destined doom that he maun dree,
When, racking at a gallows tree,*
　　He birles canny roun'.
He'll blaw na, then, up to the skies—
Swear she hath got ta Hielan' prize ;
But hing her heid—this Man o' Lies—
　　As 'twerna Kyley Broun.

---

* I heard many years after that he had sold off and left for Australia, where he actually met the doom spoken of in the rant for being concerned, along with twelve others, in the murder and robbery of a gold-digging party returning to Melbourne.

TRANENT MASSACRE.*

—:—

MAY Geordie sing dool on his throne,
An' yon red-coated minions be
A bye-word an' a warning shown,
To him wha wad enthrall the free !
But, oh ! alake, he'll ne'er come back—
The bonnie lad was joe to me !—
A madman sodger hack'd him doun,
As he cam', whislin', o'er the lea.

For gatherin' in a lawfu' cause,
To plead their plea like Scottish men,
The tyrants, traitors to all laws,
Dealt a wide country death an' pain !
O, bluidy day ! O, deadly day !
That I was born thy weird to dree—
That wrapt, O, my lad, in bluidy clay,
An' beded me with miserie.

How fairly seemed that Lammas morn,
How sweetly heard the shearer's sang,
How clear my laddie's lilt was borne—
The very hills for pleasure rang.
But ah, waes me ! baith lilt and sang
Was changed or nicht for sab an' grane ;
For mithers wailing loud and lang,
An' me for my dear laddie slain.

* By the military called out to quell a Militia disturbance, on the 29th
of August, 1797.

Some will bewail a bairnie dear,
　Was shot or butcher'd in their sight ;
A brither there—a faither here—
　In red wat death gasht grim that night.
An' thou, my laddie, evermair,
　Down to the lagging hour I dee,
For that my heart is fou an' sair,
　Will wither auld still wailing thee.